The Ghost
of
Pont Diable

The Ghost
of
Pont Diable

written and illustrated by
James Rice

EAKIN PRESS ★ Austin, Texas

FIRST EDITION

Copyright © 1996
By James Rice

Published in the United States of America
By Eakin Press
An Imprint of Sunbelt Media, Inc.
P.O. Drawer 90159 ★ Austin, TX 78709-0159

ISBN 1-57168-130-2

Library of Congress Cataloging-in-Publication Data

Rice, James, 1934–
    The ghost of Pont Diable / written and illustrated by James Rice.
      p.   cm.
    Summary: Thirteen-year-old Bois Sec and his uncle BoBo, who travel a Louisiana bayou trading goods from their houseboat, meet a mysterious old woman who claims to know where the pirate Jean Laffite buried a chest full of gold.
    ISBN 1-57168-130-2 (alk. paper) — ISBN 1-57168-109-4 Hardback.
    [1. Bayous — Fiction. 2. Louisiana — Fiction. 3. Buried treasure — Fiction. 4. Uncles — Fiction. 5. Cajuns — Fiction. 6. Orphans — Fiction. 7. Barter — Fiction.] I. Title.
    PZ7.R3634Gh 1996
    [Fic]--dc20
                         96-24041
                            CIP
                            AC

Contents

Chapter 1

Trading Day

1893

Green curtains of foliage rose high on either bank of the narrow waterway. Overhead, gray remnants of Spanish moss were draped from branch to branch wherever there was space between outcroppings of leaves. The moss decorated every available branch like tattered, filmy evening dresses gray with age. The trees, with their outstretched branches, suggested dainty old ladies standing silently in faded garments.

The man pushing the boat did not see stately old women in the surrounding landscape. He was not a romantic. For him the gray green foliage was simply a shade from the searing Louisiana sun.

The houseboat-store moved slowly through the thick bayou water. It was powered by the steady rhythmic movement of a long pole — push, lift, pause . . . push, lift, pause . . . on and on. The boat was not big for a houseboat, but it appeared too bulky for one man to handle. The man controlling the pole was not large. BoBo was smaller than average, but he propelled the boat easily. He might have been pushing a one-man pirogue for all the effort he exerted.

The houseboat was designed to ride high on the water. It displaced little more than a pirogue, which, so it was said, could float on a heavy dew. This was a necessary feature. The craft had to travel the swamps of the Atchafalaya basin, where a large body of water might only be a shallow cover over a mud bog several feet deep.

Millions of tiny particles of vegetation formed a green blanket over the surface of the unmoving stream. The water looked firm enough to support a solid weight, but it parted easily for the boat. The wake opened briefly to reveal black water and gumbo mud underneath, then it closed to unbroken green as though nothing had passed through.

A boy came from the cabin to watch BoBo perform the task he did so well. Next year Bois Sec would see his fourteenth summer. BoBo had promised to let him take a full turn at the poling stick then. He was sometimes allowed to take an oar to help control the boat when they moved through water that had a strong current, but most of their travel was through still back country bayous. The water did not move in the bayous unless the big river overflowed its banks.

The banks widened and the vegetation thinned as they rounded a bend in the stream. A small dock projected into the water from a point on the bank several yards ahead. BoBo steered toward the landing.

The solid banks bordering the waterway were used to good advantage. The houses were spaced little more than a good shout apart, but the land belonging to each house stretched back several hundred yards. The part nearest the house was cleared for garden and food crops. An intermediate area was used for stock and pasture, and the rear of each piece of land merged with the woods behind. The wooded area was used for hunting and trapping.

Most of the houses had a small landing on the water with a pirogue or skiff tied to it. The small, high-roofed houses were similar in construction. The roof extended past the front of the house to form a porch or gallery, where the family was likely to gather with friends on warm evenings. A steep outside staircase led to an overhead opening in the ceiling of the porch. The room above the gallery, extending above the house, was used by the bachelors and older boys of the family. It was called a *grenier,* following an old country custom of providing young Frenchmen of the family with separate quarters from the rest of the family.

Bois Sec tried to imagine himself in one of those houses with his own *grenier* and brothers and sisters and a *maman* who cooked the rich Cajun dishes. The people he knew seemed to pass through his life and then disappear to be seen again next trip. It was difficult to form deep relationships with people who were here today and gone tomorrow, but what his friendships lacked in depth were more than made up for in breadth. He knew people not from just one community but from dozens. He felt his relationship with *nonc* BoBo was better than any missing family of community ties.

Besides, he enjoyed a greater freedom of movement than most of the people in the sleepy bayou communities. The industrial revolution was slow in reaching the swampland. Some of the deep areas would not be touched by progress before another half century and two world wars had passed.

"Bois Sec, it's time to let the people know we're here. Fetch the horn so I can call them in," BoBo said as he threw a line over one of the projecting posts on the dock.

Bois Sec re-entered the cabin and returned holding a large horn. One end was carved to the shape of a miniature bowl and drilled in the center to form a mouthpiece.

"BoBo, I can't remember when we ain't had this ol' horn. How'd we come by it, anyway?" asked Bois Sec, looking at the horn in his hand.

"That's a special horn. There's not another in the world could be made to sound just like it. The sound in a horn gets better somehow every year it's used, and that old horn came from a great bull many years before your *papa* and your *papa's papa* and his *papa* before him were born. No one knows where the first Babin got it, but as far back as anybody can remember it's been handed down from one Babin to another. If that ol' horn could talk, oh the tales it could tell! Maybe the whole story of the bayou swamps as far back as a Babin poled a boat or made a trade. The Babin men have been traders as far as anyone can remember. It came from your *papa* to me, so it will go to you someday when you can make

4

the sounds that everyone knows should come from the Babin horn."

BoBo wanted to change the subject. The returning memories brought a tightening to his stomach, but Bois Sec pressed in with another question. "Tell me about things, *nonc* BoBo, about my *papa* and *maman* and my *tante* and how I came to you." The impact of the memories felt like a lead weight in his stomach.

"I've told you a dozen times, Bois Sec, and sometimes the words come hard."

"I want to hear it again so I can picture it like it was back then," Bois Sec responded. "I'm always afraid I'll forget something. Then it'll be like it never happened."

BoBo knew it was his duty to keep the past alive in the boy's mind. Everyone has a right to know where he or she came from. He braced himself and, with no outward show of his emotion, started the story again. "Your *maman* and *papa* were the happiest couple on the bayou when they found out you were coming. You had an older sister who died with the fever before she was a month old. She was weak from the beginning and she never really had a chance. Everything seemed to be going good before you were born. Nobody knows why, but your *maman* just didn't survive having you. You almost didn't make it yourself.

"You weren't even three years old when your *papa* went to New Orleans on a trading trip. He caught the Bronze John — yellow fever, some calls it. We didn't even get his body back, just a few belongings. They burned his body to stop any more spreading of the disease. They was a time before that hundreds of people at a time were dead on the streets from that sickness, so you can't blame them for reacting like they did. The time your *papa* got it they only lost a dozen people — ones who came in contact with a boat's crew that had it. I guess your *papa* had went aboard to check some cargo he'd ordered. They burnt the whole boat. Bronze John is something worth being scared of."

BoBo paused for a moment, then continued. "We just kind of natural came together, you and me. I might of had a boy of my own just a little older than you. My wife, your *tante* Elizabeth, came from outside. She wasn't like any girl I ever seen before or since. Light yeller hair and soft and frail she was — like a delicate flower that when it's picked out of its rightful place folds up and fades away. The swamp wasn't her place."

His voice caught in his throat. He could say no more about Elizabeth without losing his composure. He changed the direction of the story back to Bois Sec. "I guess it's partly because we both had something missing from our lives that we hit it off so good. You were stuck on after me like a shadow. Your questions and playing around and the funny things you did all day ever day was the onliest thing made life worthwhile at times.

"When your *papa* died they sent you over to your *nonc* Jean and *tante* Flo because they had other kids and a home and all the things it's good for a kid to have when he's growing up. I was given your *papa*'s houseboat, I guess because I helped him build it. One day after you'd gone to stay with Jean and Flo, I

6

was over a half day out on a trip when I looked up and there you was crawling out from behind a barrel of flour. I was goin' to take you back, but you put up such a fuss that I let you stay. I sent word back by another boatman so they wouldn't fret about where you were, and here you are! Been travelin' around on this old store boat for nigh on ten years now. That's the way it was."

Bois Sec started to voice another question, but BoBo cut in. "Come on, now, we been settin' here talkin' for more'n twenty minutes I'll bet and nobody even knows we're around. Gimme that horn, boy, and let's let people know we're ready to do some trading."

Bobo took the ancient instrument and blew the sounds by now familiar to all those who lived near the bayou. First came the low note barely higher than the croak of the giant bullfrog. The deep hollow sound seemed to hang close to the water and vibrate the underbrush. Then he tightened his lips for the high note that echoed through the treetops and back to earth. He repeated the call twice, although it was unlikely that anyone within miles around could have missed it the first time.

Bois Sec waited to take the horn as soon as BoBo had finished with it. He turned the old cow horn over in his hand, letting his fingers slide over the surface. It had the comfortable worn feel of an everyday object made smooth by many years of handling. He could almost feel the presence of all those gone but not forgotten Babin men who had held the old horn, the same way he held it.

BoBo had gone to the bow of their floating store

7

to watch for the arrival of the first of many *mamans* who would come that day to barter for the town goods that were stacked deck to ceiling on the small houseboat.

While BoBo was searching the bank, Bois Sec tried to get a sound from the horn. One day it would be his turn to continue the tradition. He would stand tall and blow it as none before him so people would know that it wasn't just a hunter in the woods — it was Bois Sec Babin. He had tried many times before and with the same result. He puffed and blew until his cheeks hurt and his ears popped. The result of his efforts was a weak sputtering sound. He tried with his lips tight and with his lips loose. A little sound came when he tightened his lips, but not enough to disturb BoBo, a few feet away.

He hung the prized old horn by its leather thong on a nail by the door and went on to join BoBo on the bow. They wouldn't have to wait long for their customers.

"Hey, BoBo, we running out of everything before you get around our way. What you do, make the detour this time?" The voice came from a heavyset woman younger than she looked. Her smile showed the beginnings of wrinkles around the corners of her eyes and mouth. She was the first of many who would come that day. First would come those on foot from nearby, then a few in buggies, and last those from across the bayou in their pirogues and skiffs.

BoBo answered, "*Ahn,* Mam Autin, how you are? You lookin' prettier every trip. How's the old man and the kids?"

10

"We all doin' jus' fine. The hens is laying and the fish is biting."

"You just come on board and make yourself to home. I got your order all bundled up for you. You look around and see if something else catches your eye." He paused and turned aside to Bois Sec. "Hey, Bois Sec, pour Mam Autin a cup of coffee while she visits and looks around."

Bois Sec poured her a half cup from the enormous pot of thick black Cajun coffee. One of his jobs was to see that each person who came aboard had a half cup of the brew. There were several refills for most, but all Frenchmen knew the normal portion was a half cup. Any more and the coffee would be cold before the cup was finished. Cajun coffee had to be sipped slowly. It could not be gulped like the thin, tepid stuff some outsiders called coffee.

Other women arrived before Mam Autin finished her first cup.

"Say, BoBo, whatcha get on this flowered cotton print now?" one asked.

"I give it to you special this time, ten cents or a dozen and a half eggs a yard. I'll give you enough to make a whole dress with trimmings for a couple of fryers."

"I'll give you three fryers and a dozen eggs for enough to make a dress for me and two dresses for the girls." The trading and bargaining went on and on. There was little hard money on the bayou. Many deals were exchanges of farm produce for wares. He would keep some of it and sell the rest in Morgan City.

"The old man been doin' some trapping. He want

11

to know what you give cash money for this bundle of mus'rat hides."

Bois Sec enjoyed it all, listening to the good-natured banter during the bargaining and catching up on all the local gossip.

"Say, BoBo, how *grandmere* Bergeron doing? Last time you were through I heard she was ailing."

"Oh, she up and around and meaner than ever again. She givin' the old man fits just like always."

"Did Suzette and Jean ever get around to jumping the broom?"

"Oh, yeah and none too soon . . ."

BoBo knew all the gossip from up and down the bayou. He knew all the young people who had gotten married or who were planning to do so. He knew of all the new births and whether they were boys or girls. He knew who had died or who was ailing since his last visit, and he knew who was fighting with whom and who was spending too much time fishing and not enough on the crops. He was a trader, newsman, and center for social gatherings all in one.

"I think I take about three yards of that blue calico and a sack of sugar for canning."

"You make a good choice. I think that's the prettiest material for the price I ever seen. Here, you take a couple extry needles and some red ribbon for the girls and some penny candy for the *bebes*."

"How much for the extrys?"

"No, no! That's lagniappe. They's no charge for the do-dads. They don't amount to nothing anyway." BoBo kept a supply of small items like penny candy, needles, hair ribbon, and trinkets to give away with the trade. The *mamans* always offered to pay as a gesture, but they knew there was no charge. BoBo reasoned that the goodwill was worth far more than the few pennies he would receive.

After he had taken care of the first wave of customers, Bois Sec went onto the bank where dozens of small kids were romping around and playing their games. Most of the women were accompanied by small children. The children that were Bois Sec's age had to stay home and take care of the chores. The little ones swarmed around him when he came ashore.

"Bois Sec, have you been to every place in the world?" a small girl asked. Bois Sec's travels made him the hero of all the youngsters.

"No, I guess we musta missed two or three places. We'll probably catch them next trip."

"Bois Sec, why don't you and BoBo let me go along this trip? I'll bet *maman* let me go. I'll ask her."

"Me and BoBo wouldn't mind having the company, but by the time we get back to Morgan City there ain't hardly enough space for us what with all the goods we trade for on board," Bois Sec answered with a smile toward the admiring barefoot boy clad in ragged bib overalls. He guessed that he probably looked like that when he first joined his *nonc* years ago.

"You and BoBo must be awful rich with all that tradin'. Does he give you all the money you want?"

Bois Sec shrugged his shoulders and smiled the way he did when he didn't want to reply or didn't know the answer. It only added to his stature in the eyes of the youngsters. It left something to the imagination.

"Do you ever wish you could stay in one place longer?" The question came from a wide-eyed little girl of less than half his mature age. His answering shrug and mock frown dismissed the question. But inside he had one of those fleeting moments when he wondered what it would be like to spend every night under a roof that didn't rock with the movement of the houseboat. The kids around him reminded him that he knew many people, but he had no one other than BoBo with whom he could share such secret thoughts.

"Bois Sec," BoBo was calling from the cabin of the boat, "we need another pot of coffee. You too busy to come and lend a hand?"

As the day wore on, the women drifted away to get back to their houses in time to do the chores and start supper. Soon the men would come by after their day's work to swap stories and tobacco plugs. The day usually ended with someone taking out a jug and a deck of cards for a long session of *burré*.

It was time for Bois Sec to straighten and secure the stock for the night. The ends of the bolts of cloth had to be tucked in and some had to be rerolled completely. The women had pulled them out to feel the fabric. No one could be expected to buy without knowing what she was getting. Fancy hairpieces and costume jewelry had to be replaced in boxes. Every piece had been carefully inspected dozens of times. Few could afford such luxuries to take home, but maybe next trip, if the hens were laying . . . well, they could wish.

BoBo never expected to sell many such items, but he always squeezed a few extras into his crowded shelves. He said it brought in a little of the outside world and gave people a special feeling. A part of his business, he said, was to sell dreams — like the dreams inspired by a small bolt of red silk that was displayed at every stop then wrapped in protective oilcloth and hidden away at the end of the day.

By the time all the old stock was straightened and the newly acquired bartered goods were stored away, Jean Pierre, the first of the men, arrived carrying two fruit jars of blackberry wine. "How're things up the bayou?" he said. "You still cheatin' all them poor Cajuns outa their money then flirtin' with their women while they out working the fields?"

BoBo answered, "What you mean workin' the fields? You out laying on the bank drowning worms all day. Say, when you gonna do something about these mosquitoes?" He slapped at one of the pesky insects.

"Now, you leave our skeeters alone! Nex' year we're gonna crossbreed 'em with chickens and see can't we get some new kind of fightin' game cocks! Hey, Bois Sec. I didna see you at first standing back there. Ain't gonna be too long till you're able to throw ol' BoBo. You give it a try yet?" Then aside to BoBo he said, "Lord, these kids sure gets away from you, don't they? Seems like one day you're changin' their pants and the next thing you know they're looking down at you."

Jean Pierre turned his attention back to Bois Sec. "Been on any more snipe hunts lately?" Bois Sec looked sheepish and the two adults broke into laughter.

Big Gaffe soon wandered in carrying a jar of

clear liquid. "Hey, Bobo, Jean Pierre, and there not so little Bois Sec. How you all? Ready for another snipe hunt? I hear they're runnin' pretty good up at Black Swamp," he laughed. "Say, Bois Sec, I got a lil something I made up for you." He winked at the adults and handed the boy a piece of carved wood, large on either end and small in the middle with a solid steel washer encircling the small section. It was obvious that the ends were much too large to allow the washer to slide off.

"You're supposed to take the washer off without breaking the wood. If you can figure it out without any help before you come back through, I'll give you a silver dollar."

Bois Sec reasoned if it were possible to get the washer on in the first place it must be possible to get it off, but he didn't see how. He didn't ask Gaffe for any clues. He knew he wouldn't get a straight answer.

Two more brawny swamp men sauntered in. "*Ahn,* how's the alligator hunting? Say les sample a lil more of that blackberry juice before it goes stale." Before the round of drinks was finished, more men appeared.

"Tiboy, how's them ol' bird dogs doin'?" someone asked.

Tiboy answered, "I just got one ol' bird dog now. He's better'n all the others put together. He looks lazy and he's got the biggest feet you ever seen on a dog. The first time I took him hunting he runs off in the grass charging around here and there. I couldn't see him, just the grass moving around where he was running. After a while everthing settles down and I

16

sees one ol' bird fly up. I hadn't no more'n shot him when another flies up and this goes on till I had eight or ten good birds, all flying up from this one place. My curiosity done got the best of me and I sneaks over to where that ol' dog was hid down in the grass. He had chased all them birds into a rabbit hole, and there he was with one of them big paws over it. Ever time I'd get ready to shoot, he'd raise that paw just enough to let one bird through."

The men nodded in mock seriousness at Tiboy's story of the incredible bird dog. Perhaps a few eyes glanced aside quickly at Bois Sec, but no one appeared willing to question the tale until Bois Sec could hold himself no longer.

"How did he get all them birds in that rabbit hole without some getting out while he chased down the others?"

First one, then another, and finally all of the men broke out in laughter until the little houseboat rocked.

Bois Sec suddenly realized that he was the victim of another of Tiboy's jokes. He grinned outwardly as required proof that he was a good sport, but inwardly he was embarrassed. It reminded him that the initiation that began with the snipe hunt would continue until he learned to detect whether the men were joking or making real talk.

He decided it would be more comfortable outside.

The early evening breeze was refreshing after the closeness of the overcrowded room of the houseboat. He arranged some bags of moss against the bulkhead to form a comfortable seat and leaned back to contemplate his situation. He yearned for the day he could be fully accepted into the crowd inside. But

18

when the time came for him to do a man's work day after day without the choice of returning to boyhood, would he still have such enthusiasm?

Back inside, others had brought wine jugs to be evaluated by the experienced wine connoisseurs present while more stories were told.

The last rays of sunlight had filtered through the canopy of moss-veiled trees outside when Gaston Daigle offered a suggestion. "BoBo, how about you get your squeeze box and make us a tune?"

Gaston was the youngest member of the group and as such he wasn't fully accepted. A Cajun was not accepted as a man just because he had reached a certain age or had married. Therefore his suggestion was ignored until it was echoed by one of the others a little later. "Yeah, BoBo, how about you show us what they're singing in the city?" Others joined in to persuade BoBo to play for them.

"I don't know, my fingers is pretty stiff from rowing and I'm out of practice," protested BoBo in a show of modest reluctance. Everyone knew he would give in, as always. He went to a battered old sea chest under the bottom shelf where he kept his most prized private possessions. There, on top of bundles of letters and paper yellow with age and alongside various other relics of the past, was a well-worn accordion. Some ivories were missing and an occasional key didn't work too well, but Bobo knew how to avoid those notes and fill in around the instrument's weaknesses. No one really noticed the difference. After a few glasses of good wine, it didn't seem to matter very much if some of the notes were a little too high or low.

Pierre "just happened" to have his fiddle out in

the buggy and Crevi filled in on the tingaling. Any mistakes were well covered. The local musicians had no difficulty picking up the new tunes because most of them were simply variations of old Cajun melodies with the words changed. BoBo had made up many of the new songs himself, but he didn't claim them. When someone asked about the origin of a song, he would say it was something he heard from down the river. He didn't care for the criticism or praise that might be his if he took credit for a song. He figured it would be simpler to remain anonymous. They played and sang the new tunes and all the old tunes everybody could remember.

Bois Sec sat on his bag of moss outside the door, listening and enjoying every moment while darkness enveloped the swamp. He was sound asleep before the lantern was lit and the cards were brought out for the *burré* game.

The voices were quiet. The only other sounds were those of the swamp — a few frogs, many insects, and every so often the sound of some large creature in the distance. A fog hung white and low over the water and swirled around the cypress trunks to give sounds a muffled hollow quality.

The cool, penetrating moisture brought Bois Sec awake with a shiver. He was too sleepy to get up and too uncomfortable to go back to sleep. He tried to curl up and squeeze close to the bulkhead to get a little warmth, but it didn't help. Finally, he went inside, unrolled a mattress, patted the moss filling smooth, and curled up under a thin blanket. The swamp sounds soon faded as the warmth allowed drowsiness to overtake him.

Chapter 2

On the Houseboat

Bois Sec awoke with the sun beaming full in his face through the open window. The rich smell of frying fish and eggs reminded him that his supper had been cold biscuits and cheese. From nearby, BoBo hummed the tunes from the night before while breakfast sizzled and crackled in a black iron skillet. Every once in a while he would chuckle to himself as he thought of the party that had just ended a while ago.

Bois Sec rolled and stacked his sleeping gear then hurried outside to splash the sleep from his eyes. The air was beginning to warm as the tropical sun flickered through the curtain of foliage and Spanish beard overhead. Some smoky wisps of fog still floated above the surface of the water in the deep shade.

BoBo welcomed Bois Sec to the world of the awake when he returned. His deep voice contrasted with his thin, wiry body. "Hey, Bois Sec, you sack out pretty early las' night. Whas' a matter, you got a touch of the ailment?"

The boy was helping himself to a generous serving of fish and eggs.

"No, I feel pretty good," he answered.

"You usually wide awake as a hooty owl till I chase you off to bed. You sure nothing wrong?" BoBo asked, scraping the rest of the skillet's contents into his plate.

Bois Sec finished chewing a large mouthful of the hot, greasy food before answering. "No, I feel real good. I bet a lot better off than you this morning. You were feeling your oats for sure las' night."

BoBo laughed at the memory. "Tha's for sure. Jean Pierre's blackberry wine was treating me jus' fine, but he didna have but two jars and we had to try ol' Gaffe's rice wine. He never did know how to make that stuff right. But when a good *voison* bring in a *ti* gift like a bottle of wine, how you gonna tell him that wine no good? Expecially when you're beating his pants off playing *burré?* That would be like rubbin' salt on a dog bite."

Bois Sec sniggered to himself at the picture conjured up. Ol' Gaffe was about six feet six and 250 pounds of pure toughness. It was said that in his prime he wrestled alligators before breakfast every morning just for the exercise. BoBo's size forced him to be a peaceful man who relied more on wit than muscle.

"The cards treat you pretty right las' night, *ahn?*" Bois Sec asked as he scraped the last morsel of food from his plate.

"Oh, fair to middling. I've done considerable

worse, but we come out a little to the good," BoBo replied in his usual understatement.

BoBo seldom lost at the old Cajun game, just as he seldom came out second best in anything he attempted. His luck probably came from the fact that he had more time on the boat to pursue such pastimes than did his many friends on the bank. But BoBo was not one to take chances with fate. He would no more sit down to a card game without his favorite luck charm tucked in the top of his left boot than he would try to go swimming in quicksand. More than once Bois Sec had known him to tie off around the bend from the next village and wait until the next day because he had seen or heard an unfavorable sign.

To those who were in constant contact with the swamp, evidence of the supernatural was too strong to be ignored. A part of BoBo respected the unseen spirits, but another part of him looked for a chance to challenge and conquer that which he felt but could not see. Deep down the fear of those other forces influenced many of his actions. He was angry at his fear, but he gave in to it by doing little things to appease the supernatural, such as carrying a rabbit's foot or hanging a polished metal cooking pan from the bow of the boat.

Everyone knew that the fearful *feu follets* were distracted by shining metal. BoBo had never said outright that the pan was placed in its unusual location for a special reason, but he had become very upset once before when Bois Sec had taken it down to store with the other utensils. After that, the boy had carefully avoided interfering with things that he did not understand.

23

BoBo pushed back from the table formed from boards thrown across two barrel tops.

"Wash up the breakfast dishes and I'll cast off," BoBo said.

Bois Sec didn't react right away.

"You hear me, Bois Sec, or are you daydreaming again?"

Bois Sec answered with a question that confirmed BoBo's speculation. "BoBo, tell me, where did I ever get a *ti* name like Bois Sec?"

The boy was probing into the old tender spot again. "Bois Sec is a special name given for a special reason. I know why that name was given you because I was the one got it started. It ain't your Christian name, of course, that's recorded in the old Bible in my sea chest —"

The boy interrupted, "What's so special about Bois Sec? That's just a old piece of dead driftwood that ain't good for nothin'."

It never got easier, recalling events from the old times, but BoBo tried to explain. "You understand that when you was a youngun so many sorrowful things had happened just one after the other — Elizabeth, your lil sister, your *maman,* then your *papa* — that I was fearing that it wasn't natural the way things was happening. Like maybe our family was hexed. The old stories say that the spirits won't bother worthless things; they just take things that people value highly. And it's said that they're pretty easy put off by names given to things. If we call something by a worthless name they say the spirits are fooled and they leave it alone. I set quite a bit of store by you, so I started calling you by about the most

24

worthless thing I could think of right off so you wouldn't get took like the others. The *ti* name caught on until everybody started callin' you Bois Sec. If you just say the sound without thinking of the meaning, it has a nice ring to it."

Bois Sec felt better when he turned to his tasks. He took the tin plates and iron skillet to the side of the boat and scrubbed them with moss and bayou water before rinsing them with fresh water from the barrel on deck. BoBo started his daily ritual of casting off the lines and poling to midstream.

Bois Sec lounged against the bulkhead and listened to the regular *kersplunk, kersplunk* of the pole lazily pushing them through the still bayou water. BoBo guided them toward a solid tangle of brush that did not appear to be an exit. But there was a small opening, and in a few minutes they might have been on another planet, so complete was their isolation.

BoBo knew exactly where every channel could be found in the maze of swamp bayous. A person unfamiliar with the South Louisiana waters would soon find himself aground on a mud bank. There was a mysterious moving quality about the swamp. Bois Sec had been this route many times before, but familiar landmarks seemed to change locations each time they traveled it. There were countless branches leading off the main channel. BoBo knew that most of them only twisted around on themselves to end in a tangle of underbrush somewhere deep in a snake-infested alligator basin or in a choking field of water lilies. Bois Sec knew that BoBo could find a channel of deep water where there appeared only mud and grass. He had the ability to find solid ground across a stretch of trembling swamp ground where a mis-step could sink a man to his shoulders in mud. Much of the swamp was covered by a thin crust of soil hiding the bog underneath. One had to know the look of the soil and which vegetation grew on solid ground and which covered only a thin layer of soil.

The slow moving boat was so much a part of the swamp that many creatures on the bank simply gave it a passing curious glance. They sensed no threat, and went about their business.

A thin, graceful heron was poised seemingly motionless in the shallow water some distance away. He was staring intently at an object in the edge of the grass. But the long-legged swamp bird was not motionless. His whole body was moving very slowly toward the hidden object. In a blur of movement the long beak thrust forward into the grass and returned with a frog impaled on its tip. The heron tossed the unfortunate creature into the air and caught him with practiced ease farther between his beaks. With a few juggling movements of his head and neck, he forced the still-wriggling frog down his skinny throat. At the conclusion of his savage breakfast the heron flew to the craggy branch of a fallen gumwood tree projecting from the water. He watched the scene through beady little scarlet eyes as BoBo push-poled the little craft through his territory.

Bois Sec knew there were areas of the swamp where no man had ever gone. He wondered if somewhere in those gloomy depths there were creatures as yet unknown by man that could gobble up a man with the same ease that the heron did away with the frog. An ever-so-slight tremor touched his spine at the thought. Strange stories came out of the swamp.

27

At any given moment the peaceful swamp hid a thousand violent life and death struggles. Millions of creatures, ranging from tiny insects to giant fifteen-foot alligators, constantly moved, waited and struggled to survive in the quiet backwater country. Man was the most alien of creatures to try to adapt to the hostile environment of the deep swamp land.

Bois Sec had great respect for the dangers, but he had lived with the risks since birth. Like everyone who had spent their lives in the swamp, he and BoBo knew what would happen to people who ignored the hidden dangers of the Louisiana wilderness. They knew about children who had waded too far or fallen into the bayou to be snapped up in a single bite by an alligator, grown men who had arms and legs torn off by the same beasts, people of all sizes who had carelessly disturbed the deadly cottonmouth, people who had fallen victim to the deadly Bronze John or other equally fatal swamp ailments, those who had lost lives and property in the ferocious hurricanes and devastating floodwaters from the nearby Mississippi, men who had been sucked into treacherous bogs and were never seen again.

Perhaps the thing most feared was beyond explanation. A person could be well and happy one week then one day he would walk into the swamp and not return, or he might withdraw into a period of depression from which there was no release until he was dead or driven to madness. Some people said that the cause of the malady was the combination of loneliness, weariness of the struggle against constant harshness, and a feeling of futility. BoBo did not understand these explanations. He did not see how a man could give up no matter what odds were against him. He reasoned that the forces that would cause a person to give in to swamp madness were outside the body.

BoBo had heard many stories of the awesome powers of unseen forces in the swamp. They told of the many restless spirits of those who had not received proper burials and how they were doomed to roam the watery wasteland until they were allowed to return to eternal rest, and how they could be recalled by certain ancient voodoo rites and do one's bidding. It was said that the spirits could be easily angered by certain human actions and that there were certain methods of appeasing them.

BoBo did not openly show his fear of these mysterious forces. They were like any other dangerous situations in the swamp. One had to be aware of them and know the proper precautions, then he could go about his business. He felt that if he could openly confront and defeat these forces just once, he would never again feel the fear that annoyed him.

Sometimes Bois Sec and BoBo would spend hours without speaking a word. Words were not necessary between the two. BoBo finally broke the silence.

"It looks like a good place to catch a couple a catfish up ahead. You wanna bait three, four line while I push over and make fast the mooring?"

"Ahn?" Bois Sec had been halfway between a daydream and a real dream when he was aroused. He recognized the cove where they had stopped several times before. He prepared the fishing line and hooks before BoBo finished tying to.

"What time you think we get to Beaux Croix?"

"We ain't got no hurry. We fry up a good mess of fish, open a can of peaches, and settle in for a good night's rest before we hit the bank tomorra. There's no need to get to town at night unless it's a big town. Beaux Croix done rolled up and gone to bed at sundown. You can't go callin' on people at the wrong time. Sure they come out, rush through and pick up their orders and go home. You mebe make a few more stops, but you take all the fun out of it. We jus' take our time like always."

Bois Sec wasn't in a hurry to get to town. He finished baiting the lines and tossed them over the side while BoBo continued.

"I seen plenty people with more money, but what good is all that stuff when you can't get up and go when you want to? What good is money when you gotta be a slave to get it? There ain't nothing wrong with money, now. I'd like to have a couple bushels of it if they weren't no strings tied on behind it. I'd buy me a steamboat about a hunnert feet long and paint it all yeller with some red and gold trimmin'. I'd run cold beer in the pipes and play *burré* all night ever night. We'd dress fit to kill and put on the airs like you never seen."

Bois Sec laughed at this turn of BoBo's speech, but he knew such things didn't happen to people in the swamp. Neither of them knew about such things except as they saw them in the picture magazines.

Bois Sec joined in BoBo's fantasies. "I'd get me a big soft chair all stuffed with feathers and hire me somebody to hold my fishing pole for me, and I'd just sit in that chair on deck all day watching him pull in the fish," he said.

They both laughed at the picture of two dandies living in luxury with servants to do their bidding. It was such a complete contrast to the real image — their coarse, homespun clothes and faces weather-beaten by outdoor living. Their imaginary trips could not take them away from the basics of their life — a boat and the familiar bayou surroundings. They were born to the swamp.

BoBo looked at Bois Sec and wondered what it would be like to live a different life, one that was more civilized. A boy needed to know something more than the narrow swamp life. There was a whole world the boy was missing. On the other hand, the boy was learning some things books couldn't teach. BoBo had known educated men who wouldn't last a day in the swamp. Books didn't always teach common sense. Bois Sec would be able to take care of himself when he reached manhood.

Bois Sec was curious about the world beyond the swamp, but he couldn't imagine he and BoBo being together any other way. Everything they did was connected to the houseboat and its familiar route. He dreamed sometimes of doing new things and going new places with BoBo. The main thing, he figured, was to keep their freedom.

Both of their musings were cut short by the sight of one of the corks bobbing, then disappearing completely under the water. A second cork reacted the same way. The first fish was more than enough for the two of them, so BoBo threw the second one back.

"If you take more than you need from the land, it

won't give it back when you need it," BoBo said. To him the swamp was a great living being with emotions. It watched over its creatures or punished them as it saw fit.

Like most Cajuns, BoBo considered himself a good Catholic, but God was so distant and the swamp was so near. In his mind there was no conflict between the church and his feeling about the swamp. God was perhaps the easiest swamp spirit to appease. BoBo wore his crucifix faithfully and confessed to the priest occasionally, when it was handy to do so.

Bois Sec cleaned the fish while BoBo started the fire and readied the skillets and pans. They had barely settled down to the meal when they became aware of a tapping on the side of the boat.

"You tie that skiff up tight?" asked BoBo.

"You know it. My knots ain't slipped yet, besides the skiff on the other side," Bois Sec answered through a full mouth.

Again the tapping, more insistent this time.

"We musta snagged a piece of driftwood," BoBo said as they continued eating.

A few moments later the sound occurred again. This time there could be no mistake. Someone was banging on the side of the boat.

They both rose and went quickly to the side.

Chapter 3

Swamp Woman

In the deepening shadows alongside the boat was a pirogue with a lone passenger. They had to look closely to see that it was indeed a passenger in the small craft. It looked more like a twisted piece of driftwood heavily hung with dried moss and matted with moldy leaves.

The fading light revealed an ancient woman garbed in a single, threadbare gray garment covered with dark patches. Her long, matted gray hair matched the clothing. The skin on her face looked like weathered dry leather stretched tight over bones. A network of deeply etched wrinkles filled the hollows of her face. Her sharp little eyes bore through each of her hosts in turn.

It was several seconds before anyone broke the silence. Her stacatto voice rasped out from between widely spaced brown teeth. "A fine pair of French gentlemen you be. Ain't cha gonna even let a old woman come on board for a minute to rest her bones?"

BoBo and Bois Sec were surprised that such a creature could speak and doubly amazed at the energy and force in her voice. BoBo wanted to tell her to find some place else to rest, but that would have been a violation of Cajun hospitality. One never sent a visitor on his way in the swamp near nightfall. If he were to commit such a deed he would never sell another dollar's worth of merchandise on the bayou.

"Why sure, ol' lady, lemme help you tie up alongside, then you come on up and have a bite with us."

Before BoBo could finish speaking she grasped the low railing and vaulted aboard. She went directly to the stove and ate from the skillet. Only the bonier pieces of fish remained, but that didn't slow her. She started at one end and chewed through meat, bones, and fins to the other end. She picked up three slices of thick homemade bread and swabbed all the grease from the skillet. Without pausing, she poured half the can of peaches into the skillet and just as quickly gulped them.

The man and boy continued their meal in silence while they watched the food disappear. When she finished the meal, Bois Sec poured her the usual half cup of scalding Cajun coffee. She finished it with one swallow and poured herself another cup, this time filled to the brim. The second cup was nursed in true Cajun fashion.

In the uneven half light, every wrinkle of her face was accented. The gnarled, protruding bones of her face caught reflections from the flickering lantern to project a mysterious ghostly image. Her

piercing eyes glared first at one and then the other from behind the steaming coffee cup cradled in her bony hands.

Bois Sec wished she would leave, but at the same time he felt a certain pity for her. He sensed an element of femininity under the hard exterior. Perhaps a brief wavering in her stare suggested that her roughness was a shield she had erected in order to survive in the swamp. She showed no inclination to move from her comfortable resting place.

"I sure be much obliged to you two boys for puttin' up with a poor ol' lady what's a bit down on her luck right now. Them vittles was sure worth talking about. You don't by some offhand chance just happen to have a extry twist of terbacky? I just run out day before yesterday. Been chewin' sasfras roots, but that don't cure the cravin'. Hey, youngun, you get yourself out to my pirogue and fetch me that ol' toe sack throwed up in back there."

Bois Sec went to the pirogue that was tied to the railing. In the deepening gloom alongside the boat he had difficulty at first seeing the parcel. It was the only thing in the pirogue, except for a short oar and the poling stick. The bag was heavy enough to be hard to carry with one hand, but it was small when one considered that it probably held everything the old woman owned. It seemed to be made of the same material and had the same musky odor as the clothing worn by the old lady. What secrets of a lifetime in the swamp could be held in one small bag? Could the single bag be all she had to show for her efforts?

Many questions popped into Bois Sec's mind as he struggled to put the bag on board the houseboat.

If the old woman had a place to go — a home, or friends or possessions — she would not be wandering alone in the swamp so late and so far from other people. Did a similar fate await others who gave themselves to a life in the swamp? Would she someday perish in its depths with no one knowing or caring? He suddenly felt anxious to get back inside with the others.

BoBo had offered a twist of tobacco to their guest. She had taken a generous chaw and from somewhere in the folds of her garment brought out an untrimmed homemade corncob pipe. BoBo had produced his own homemade pipe, but its carefully carved bowl showed the effects of many hours of painstaking handicraft. The design was polished to a smooth, even patina.

When Bois Sec returned with the old woman's parcel, he found the room thick with strong, rich tobacco smoke. It was the first time he had ever seen anyone smoke and chew tobacco at the same time.

She took the bag from him and reached deep into its contents.

"You boys sure done me a good turn. I ain't got much, but I want to repay the favor partway if I can."

"Oh no, there ain't no need for that," protested BoBo. "Why, I can't count the times I've been caught out on the bush at night and had to bust in on somebody uninvited. I can't take nothing for doin' no more than a man's obliged to do."

She ignored his protest and sat a half-gallon crock jug on the barrel top between them. When BoBo hesitated, she hooked a forefinger into the handle, balanced the jug on her forearm, and tilted it to her lips. The jug was considerably lighter when she sat it down. Many favors could be refused, but it would have been a severe breach of Cajun etiquette to refuse the offer of a friendly drink. It became a matter of honor now to keep up with his female guest.

"Here you are. You may as well cut some o' that gumbo mud from your gullet and clear your pipes," she said, pushing the jug toward him.

"Well, I just can't rightly turn down a little drop of the grape since you put it that way," he said, turning up the jug for a healthy shot. The first taste proved it was not related to fruit of the grape. It was a bolt of pure white lightning. The roots of his hair tightened on his scalp, the heat built up inside his eardrums, and he felt the top layer of membrane dissolving in his throat. But he could not put down the jug until he had taken at least two full swallows. It took all his self-control to keep from coughing or strangling. Experience had taught him to take a few shallow, well-spaced breaths before filling his lungs completely. It was easy to understand why the old woman had a low, raspy voice. BoBo's own voice was now a little lower and huskier when he spoke.

"*Sacre!* That was one good drink!" he lied, but he knew on the next drink he would purse his lips and sip instead of gulping. He would have trouble keeping up with the old woman even if he matched her sip for gulp.

The jug continued to pass back and forth, with the old woman getting the larger share each time. The drinks did not dim the sharpness in her eyes. She showed no outward signs of drunkenness, but she did become very talkative. As she talked she became more intense. Her eyes bore through her small audience with a stare that dared them not to listen, even if her statements were sometimes unbelievable.

"I've been watching you boys — you can tell a lot about a body just watching," she said. "I been watching people all my life. There's them that are nice when the goin' is good and then they don't know you when it ain't. Then there's them who are just pure mean all the time. Some others are changeable people. They are just what they think people expect them to be. When they be with good people they're good; when they be with bad people they're bad. Then there's double people who spend their lives lettin' on to be one kind of people when deep down they're somebody else completely. Usually something happens sooner or later to bring out that second person that's really been there all the time."

She stopped to take another long drink from the jug and paused a few moments to let it settle. Her speech became more precise as she continued.

"Other people don't know how to be nobody but their natural selves. They ain't mean and they ain't exactly extry good. If they eat fish on Friday and chicken on Sunday when they poor they gonna eat fish on Friday and chicken on Sunday when they rich. If they calculate to like a body when everybody else like him they still gonna like that body after everybody else throws him to the dogs. Natural people knows how to get along with theirselves and they knows how to get along with others."

She took another pull from the jug and didn't seem to notice when BoBo didn't take his answering sip. She continued, warming to a point she hadn't made yet.

"I ain't too sure what kind of a person I am, but I think you boys are just what you are. I judge a person by how I feels about them. They either feels right or they ain't no amount of convincing or later happenings can change that first feeling. I ain't never been wrong when I've had that feeling as strong as I got it now.

"I'm a old woman without much left. I'm getting too old to finish some of the things I've started. Sometimes a person got to figure she can't do all she set out to do, so she may as well find somebody she can trust to carry out what she started. She has to trust her secrets to somebody, else she pass on and they gets lost to everybody from then on. It just ain't right to let them things what people has worked for get lost forever just because she can't have them herself. I'm reaching the point where I got to rely on my judgment and trust somebody. My bones is gettin' stiffer every year. What I'm gonna tell you I ain't told another soul that's still alive today . . ." She hesitated a moment. "I know where ol' Jean Laffite buried a sea chest full of gold!"

She stopped again to tip the jug and let her statement sink in. Up to this point both BoBo and Bois Sec had just been enduring her speech. Now they became alert and intent on what she said. They were both filled with excitement. They tried hard to hide it lest they scare her off. BoBo was so shocked, he took a full gulp of the white lightning before he realized what was happening.

The bayou country was full of stories about the

pirate Jean Laffite. The notorious pirate was said to have left numerous caches of booty at various points up and down the Louisiana coast. Hundreds of men had made treasure-hunting expeditions. A few made it their life's work. They took regular jobs only when necessary to raise enough money to pay for the next expedition. A few others had bought or homesteaded land in the Barataria Bay or Terrebonne Bay area so that they could conduct careful detailed searches of all likely hiding places. Those people became upset when outsiders made digging expeditions on their property. A few people had actually found evidence that the treasures existed, usually in the form of a few coins washed ashore.

It was a matter of record that for some years the infamous pirate had used Gran Terre Island off Barataria Bay as his headquarters, primarily because there were so many well-hidden navigable streams in the immediate area. It was easy for him to raise anchor on short notice and elude capture in one of the hundreds of nearby streams or coves. He had made it his business to know every one of them. Laffite reportedly brought in scores of ships loaded with booty. Because he was afraid to leave all his booty in one place, he was said to have hidden part of his treasure in different places in the nearby swamp-lands.

Practically everyone in South Louisiana knew someone who knew someone who had a map that had been handed down by Laffite himself. Of course, most of the stories were false. But true or false, each story created excitement and produced a fresh crop of treasure hunters. All the reports of treasure were

revealed in an air of great secrecy, but within a short time everyone within miles knew every detail of the original story plus additions that had developed in the retelling.

BoBo had heard many treasure stories in his travels, but he had never personally known anyone who had found anything. He was naturally skeptical, but at the same time he could not help being excited. The main cause of his excitement, whether he realized it or not, was the chase itself — of doing something that others had tried and failed to do.

All his life Bois Sec had heard tales of the infamous Jean Laffite and his buried treasure. He was curious to see it to find out what made men do the things they did to get it.

Both BoBo and Bois Sec leaned forward to hear the old woman's next words, but she was in no hurry to continue. She leaned back and chuckled slightly as though she were reminded of some long past incident. They did not want to betray their anxiety, but it showed in their faces and actions. They wisely decided to let the story unroll naturally without pushing the old woman. She ignored her curious audience, took another drink, and continued as though talking to herself.

"A few years ago, before I came to the bayous, I was quite a beauty, you know. There wasn't a young buck around who wouldn't look twice when I walked by."

She seemed to have forgotten her earlier announcement about the treasure.

"I lived for a spell up in New Orleans in them days," she grinned, breaking her face into a thousand new wrinkles. "I met a lot of people — nice people, all kinds people. Had myself a lot of fun. There wasn't no yesterdays and no tomorrows, just one big today. *Papa* always seemed to have enough money to pay the bills so I didn't have to work. He'd get on me ever once in a while to get a job, so I'd hire on somewhere or other for a week or so before I got fired or quit. Steady work interfered with my play. We'd eat in the fanciest restaurants and dance all night." She refilled her pipe and took another drink.

The image of this coarse, dried-up old shell of humanity made her story all the more incredible. She looked like a person who had grown up and become a part of the swamp. She looked into the distance with the same intensity as she had looked at her hosts earlier — as though she were piercing time to witness again these scenes from her youth. Her eyes softened and her body relaxed somewhat as though she had seen through the barriers of time to another existence.

She continued her story.

"I met this boy, Henri. A real sport, he was. They wasn't nothing real serious between us. We had both been with the same crowd for two or three days and it seemed we kind of got throwed together since the others were already paired off. He was a real fancypants gentleman and he liked to gamble like nobody I ever seen. For a while there it seemed like he couldn't lose at anything — horses, cards, dice. Whatever he bet on, he was coming out ahead. That last night of the spree he got into this card game. He liked to have me stand close by — said I brung him luck. And the way things was goin' I was beginning to believe it myself. Every card he turned up seemed to be the right one.

"Then he started turning up bad hands. Instead of holding off on the betting until his luck changed, he just kept doubling up. Why, in one hand he stayed in and tried to bluff his way through with a pair of treys. When you're losing money, it seems to always go out a lot faster than it comes in when you're winning. Anyway, once he started to lose it wasn't more than about three hour until he was scraping bottom. He excused himself for one hand and motioned me over to one side. In his very gentleman-like way he said that he never had asked nobody, man or woman, for charity but he knew beyond a doubt that if he could get back into the game for another hand or two his luck would change. He made it clear he didn't want no handout but that he would like to have a little loan. In return he said he would leave in my hands a very valuable paper as security.

"Now, I said I'd be more than glad to loan him whatever I had on me but I didn't really need no paper. His pride wouldn't have it no other way, though, and he gave me his paper. It was sealed up in a heavy envelope with some kind of wax holding the flap down. He said I was on no account to open it unless he lost. It didn't make no real difference to me. I didn't put too much stock in sealed envelopes, but I went along with it anyway."

She stared off in the distance as she remembered. "I had a considerable sum on me at the time. He took it and lost it about two hands later trying to fill an inside straight. I went over to the cashier, who knew me pretty good, and gave him a marker for another considerable sum, which he lost almost as fast. When he got up from the table he looked like he'd have to improve a good bit to feel good enough to die. I never seen anybody so down at the mouth. I offered him his envelope back, but he acted like that was just about the most insulting thing anybody could do. There weren't no doubt that he put a lot of stock in whatever was in that envelope, but he wouldn't have nothing at all to do with it.

"Gamblers and gentlemens is funny people," she offered to explain. "They got their own kind of honor or pride or whatever you want to call it. They got their own set of rules and they feel that if they break one of them rules they're disgraced for life. I reckon we all got rules we set up for ourselves. Most of 'em is just common sense, but gentlemens and gamblers' rules seem kind of silly to me.

"Anyway, this boy, the first and onliest person I ever met by the name Henri that sounded like he said it, he stomped out like a mad bull. I think he was more upset at me trying to give him his envelope back than he was about losing the money in the first place. I'll bet if I'd been a man he'd knocked me down on the spot or worse. I put his envelope up. I figured he'd cool off after a while and be back for it, but I never seen him again. Heard a year or so later that he'd got hisself killed in a gunfight, probably one of his 'affairs of honor,' as he called them."

BoBo and Bois Sec were beginning to get impatient, but they knew better than to try to rush her. It was almost as though the old woman were under a spell. She paused for what seemed a long while. Bois Sec thought he saw tears form in the corners of her eyes. It was hard to tell for sure because the light was uncertain and the deep wrinkles would have swallowed them as soon as they formed. She sagged visibly and looked very tired as she continued, somewhat slower than before.

"It sure was funny the way things happened after that last night that Henri left. My luck changed about the same time his did. *Papa* made some bad business deals and lost about everything he had pretty soon after that, and he broke down and died. All he left in the end was a pile of bills that I couldn't pay. I finally opened Henri's envelope; I wasn't really expecting too much. I found some writing that I couldn't make out on pages that looked like they had been tore out of some kind of book and some letters. Besides that, there was some kind of drawing like a map on old thick yeller paper. I made out a few of the words on the pages — enough to figure out that it was writ in French. They was a lot of people around who could talk French — I talked it myself — but there weren't many, myself included, who could read it or write it. There was even fewer a body could trust. It took a few days, but by asking around I found somebody to tell me what it meant.

"To sum everything up, the letter was to Henri from his uncle twice removed from somewhere in France. It claimed that he, the uncle, was some kind of relative, a grandson or something or other, of Jean Laffite hisself, and since he was getting pretty old he was passing the papers on to Henri as the only one of his relatives who might believe them and do something about it. The pages was from a ship's log, and they told how on such and such a date Jean had bur-

47

ied a load of treasure at a point marked on the map. The log said that it was 'very regrettable' that a crew member had to be killed and buried with the treasure because he was a spy. It makes a body wonder how and why he really came to his end.

"Several people down the line, including Henri's uncle, twice removed, had tried to get the treasure. But every time they tried, something bad happened. The first time Henri's uncle went, he had been not more than a youngun. The group left him in the boat while they went ashore. That's the last he recollected until a few days later. Some shrimp fishermen found him floating around in the skiff in the bay, scared half out of his wits and not even remembering what it was had scared him. They looked all over the place but never found a trace of those who had gone ashore. He tried again after he growed up, but his boat hit a snag or something and turned over. His oldest boy drowned and he just barely managed to get out alive hisself. He never tried again. He mighta sent somebody, but I has my doubts.

"The man reading the papers to me was pretty impressed. He checked it out as best he could in books and records, and he took the map and re-marked it with the names of places we call them now. Laffite had his own names for places, but by putting the map side by side with all kinds of newer maps we finally figured it out."

The woman looked very old and very tired. She appeared to be shrinking within her skin. Her words were beginning to drag, but she was determined to tell the story to its end. Her half-smoked pipe was cold in her hand, forgotten. She tipped the jug up and drained the last few ounces. Temporarily revived, she continued.

"That blasted envelope and its cursed papers and that damned map. I've wished a million times I'd never seen them. I've spent all these years, seen my youth go. And I've seen so many awful things, so many good men dead because of that map. I almost had it once — almost had my hands on it. It's hard to talk about it. Strange things happen around where that treasure is buried. I've been there, I've seen it — enough to make a thousand men rich for life — and then had something go wrong so I couldn't get out with it. Always something would go wrong, like a boat springing a leak, or twisting my leg, or one thing or another so I'd wind up feeling lucky I got out myself. It just ain't natural the way something always seems to happen to anybody ever time they gets close to it.

"And that ain't all," she whispered. "There's a spooky feeling about the whole place, like something unnatural had control of what was happening. Strange, strange . . . I can't tell how or why. I'd be happy dying today if I knowed somebody got in there to where that treasure is and stole it away from whatever evil force is guarding it. It's like a feeling in my bones that that evil thing, whatever it is, is goin' to haunt me in my grave through all eternity if I don't take something from him to break his hold on me. I'm too old and ain't got the strength to make it again myself, and there ain't nobody I can trust anymore."

It was as though she were calling on some last reserve of energy to continue. In that same surge of vitality, as fast as a cat catches a mouse, she grasped the right wrist of Bois Sec and the left wrist of BoBo. Bois Sec recoiled, but the cold, hard grip of those bony fingers was too strong. She crossed their wrists and seemed to pierce to the depths of their souls with her cutting eyes. She spoke again.

"Like I said before, I got a feeling about you boys — a feeling like I might not get again about any living soul in the short time I got left. I'm askin' you to finish what I been trying to do all these years. I don't want no big reward, just a token from the grave where the treasure's buried so I can rest in peace when my time comes." Her voice was like a rasping, chilling swamp wind penetrating to the depths of the spine. "By all the black spirits of the swamp I'm pledging you to finish my task for me, else as I am haunted from the grave so shall I return to haunt you from the grave through all eternity. So I swear by all that is good and by all that is evil. So I swear . . . so I swear . . ." Her voice was trailing off to a hoarse whisper, but the meaning of her words echoed through the mind like a voice shouting from the treetops to the underbrush for all creatures of the night to hear and heed.

The two strained to hear if any more words were forthcoming before she collapsed into unconsciousness, still sitting more or less upright. Only then did she release her vise-like grip from the wrists of her captives.

Two minutes later she was snoring loudly. It was obvious that there would be no reviving her until her rest was complete.

It had been a long, tiring evening. Soon all aboard were in the netherworld of sleep.

Chapter 4

A Narrow Escape

BoBo opened his eyes too fast and a sunbeam exploded through the back of his skull. He squinted one eye open a crack in order to identify a recurring banging noise on the deck. When the dazzling blur gradually came into focus, he discovered that the sound was only the *drip-drop* of water falling off a leaf onto the boat.

The inside of his mouth felt as if it had been pickled and stuffed with cotton. The white lightning of the previous evening was responsible for his condition. He closed his eyes tightly, wrapped a blanket around his head to muffle the noise, and blindly reached out to shake Bois Sec awake. He rasped one word, "Coffee!" and rolled over to try to revive himself as slowly and painlessly as possible.

Bois Sec had known BoBo to suffer hangovers a few times in the past, but he rarely let himself be caught off guard. Last night was the exception. The

old woman's brew had been more potent than anything BoBo had drunk before.

Bois Sec prepared the strong coffee and started to awaken BoBo when something on the table caught his attention.

"BoBo!" he yelled. "BoBo, wake up! Wake up! Come see what I found!"

"*Grrl, mfmpft, wmmft,*" BoBo muttered and slowly unwound himself from the blanket to see what the disturbance was. On the table was a folded piece of heavy yellowed paper and on top of it was a gold coin. Engraved into one side of the coin was the image of a large cross and on the other was a shield containing some illegible letters and a strange horse-like animal that neither of the pair could identify. They looked around for the old woman, but she had disappeared along with her pirogue. The only evidence she left was the paper on the table and the empty crock jug. Scrawled across the paper was a barely legible message: "If n U fin wat yur lukkin for i'l b arownd to git my shaire — gud luk —" It was unsigned.

Bois Sec watched BoBo, his hangover apparently forgotten, as he carefully unfolded the ancient parchment. The paper was soiled and worn from much handling and age. It was the map the old woman had described the previous night.

BoBo took a cup of thick black coffee and settled down to study the map in detail.

"You think you might be able to figure it out?" asked Bois Sec, peering over his shoulder.

"This 'X' out here on the edge of Pont Diable must be where it's buried," BoBo pondered. "Trouble is, there ain't really a place called Pont Diable any-more. It probably got changed around in the hurri-cane and floods in '56. That whole area got messed up then. The 'X' seems to be near a big oak tree that's lined up with two great big cypress trees to the north, according to the writing."

A map of South Louisiana that had been accu-rate three or four decades ago could be very difficult to decipher. The bayou waters had a way of changing with time. Storms pushed Gulf waters over low swamps and marshes to clog old channels and create new ones. From the other direction the Mississippi River poured flood waters into the Atchafalaya ba-sin every few years with the same effect.

"If the land's changed around, what makes you think the trees is still there?" Bois Sec wondered.

"The fact that the main tree is a oak is a good sign. Oak trees will live for hundreds of years. They can stand up to about anything and they just grow on high ground away from the salt marsh. So what-ever is buried near it would still be there. Anything buried in the marsh itself would sink to the center of the earth before it stopped. The cypress tree, it'll still be there unless somebody's hauled it away. Any other tree will rot away when it dies, but that ol' cy-press won't rot. The termites won't bother it, even the woodpeckers won't touch it. I guess a cypress lasts forever even after it's dead," mused BoBo.

"But if they's not even a place called Pont Diable now, how we gonna find it?" asked Bois Sec.

"As far as I can tell it's a little spot over here on the west coast of Barataria Bay north of Grand Terre. I can tell that by starting from the 'X' and

54

working back to the names of places I know. When it comes right down to it, though, there just ain't no way we can find it that I can see without getting somebody who knows that part of the country better than we do to help us."

BoBo continued to study the map until past the time for them to get under way. Bois Sec stared at the paper for a while, trying to connect what he saw on the paper with BoBo's words, but he couldn't make any sense of it. The paper itself seemed to hold a force of its own, a spell left over from departed spirits of those whose blood had been spilled in its behalf. He bent close to the yellowed paper, and a faint chill slid up his back. Being close to it suddenly made him very uneasy.

He went outside to find other ways to amuse himself. A frog entertained him with a staring contest for several moments then turned his attention to a dragonfly on a nearby leaf. Bois Sec tied four hollow reeds together with thin vines and saw grass to make a miniature raft. A broad leaf held upright by a thin grass stem wedged between the reeds formed a fragile sail. He added several small forked sticks for a crew, and suddenly an imaginary Jean Laffite was ready to set sail on another voyage of conquest.

It was fun sometimes to forget about having to grow up. Bois Sec's imagination helped fill the void of loneliness he sometimes felt when they were alone in the deep swamp and BoBo was busy with other matters. It helped relieve the hard realities of facing the swamp day after day.

The bold, imaginary pirate made several stops

along the bank, picking up booty in the form of golden flower petals, pieces of bark, and a few pebbles. He returned to his hideaway in the twisted roots of a large cypress tree half in the water, half on the bank. In the water offshore a monstrous ship (in the form of a partially submerged log) drifted slowly toward the pirate's hideout.

Bois Sec was so absorbed in helping his pirate friend hide his ill-gotten treasure that he did not see a glazed eye move in its protruding bulge on top of the log and a slight side-to-side swishing movement in its wake. It moved like no log in nature.

Bois Sec quickly dug a shallow hole in the mud, glancing up frequently to observe the approaching man-o-war. When the last of the treasure was safely in the hole, he hastily covered it and made ready to aid the pirate in his flight from the enemy vessel. Bois Sec pushed the vessel out from the bank to allow the sail to catch a trace of breeze, but the still, heavy air did not move the fleeing pirate's ship. Bois Sec stepped into the water to push the vessel into the same current that moved the log, but it still did not move beyond the point where it was pushed. He stepped further into the water to force the craft into midstream. At this point, the log disappeared beneath the surface.

The boy gave the boat a quick boost, and almost immediately the log sprang from the water with large jaws open wide to show flashing double rows of wicked, curved teeth. In an instant they had banged closed, crushing their target.

The largest reptile in the swamp had no natural enemies in his home territory except man. The huge

alligator that had been present in the cove at the arrival of the houseboat had never met a hostile man, so he had seen no reason to flee when the intruders came. As far as he was concerned, he was master of all creatures.

He had lounged in the underbrush on the mud bank during the late evening and through the night. When the sun started beating through the foliage, he had slid into the muddy water. Like other reptiles, the alligator does not like direct sunlight. His body cannot cope with extreme temperatures. So he lay in the shallow water with only his nostrils and bulging eyes above the surface when the distraction on the bank had caught his attention. His long, scaled tail had propelled him toward the new disturbance.

When the boy had entered the water, the alligator had sensed the possibility of a fresh meal. As Bois Sec stepped farther into the water, the king of the swamp had submerged and swum quickly toward his target. The alligator has a keen sense of smell, but he relies more on his sharp vision and sensitive hearing when he gets near his objective. At the last moment, before swinging his gaping jaws upward and sideward, a splashing movement in front of the primary target had diverted his aim to the new sound. The great jaws had crunched together on Jean Laffite's tiny frail craft, transforming ship, crew, and sail into a mouthful of splinters.

Before the beast could recover his balance, Bois Sec was on the bank, moving rapidly in the opposite direction. The huge alligator was on the bank in a moment, his great body held as high above the ground as his stubby legs would allow. He moved at amazing speed, considering his awkward shape, but the boy leaped onto the safety of a low hanging branch just ahead of the snapping jaws.

Bois Sec held on tightly. He was afraid that his trembling would break the branch. A quivering weakness began in his abdomen and spread to his toes and fingertips. Only instinct gave him the strength and control to maintain his grasp on the branch. As soon as his body calmed down, he climbed higher. It wasn't necessary. The alligator had a limited reach.

When it became apparent that no meal would be forthcoming, the creature made his way back into the water. Soon he was sliding through the thin mud in search of other game. His little mind did not allow for reflections or regrets. It was another incident in another day, no more.

Bois Sec stayed in the tree for a long while after the alligator left. For a moment he had forgotten one of the first rules for survival. He had allowed his fantasies to override his awareness of the dangers of the swamp.

Chapter 5

The Invitation

"Bois Sec!" came the familiar voice from the store boat. "Bois Sec, where you at? Walk yourself this way and throw off them lines. Bois Sec?" he repeated upon getting no reply. "It's time to move on!"

Bois Sec refrained from answering as long as he dared. He didn't plan to tell BoBo of his misadventure, and he was afraid his voice would betray his emotions. His stomach felt queasy and his throat was tight. When he finally answered, his voice was surprisingly husky. "I'm coming!"

"Hurry up, the sun's getting high."

"Keep your pants on, I'm coming," answered Bois Sec with more confidence now.

"Don't get sassy. Where you been anyway?"

"Down yonder a ways."

"What you been doin' that you couldn't answer?"

"Just foolin' around."

BoBo laughed and Bois Sec felt easier.

"Boy, if things work out we're goin' to get to do some fancy foolin' around before too many sunsets from now," said BoBo.

Bois Sec was relieved that BoBo was too involved with thoughts of treasure hunts to be concerned with his recent whereabouts.

BoBo continued. "We're going to finish this run double fast and find somebody to help us figure out this map. It's sure got me stumped. That's going to be some kind of a problem. We can't just go in and tell everybody we see: 'We got a treasure map here, any you folks want to help us do some deciphering?' We got to go real slow and sneaky, else we got everybody and their dog follering us around trying to get in on a good thing. Ain't no good can come out of a lot of people poking around where they don't know what they're looking for in the first place."

As they talked they prepared for casting off. In a matter of minutes BoBo was poling through the narrow bayou stream. Bois Sec found a comfortable spot on a coil of rope on the bow. He leaned back and tried to doze, but every time he nearly fell asleep a vision of the great snapping alligator jerked him to full wakefulness. Once, when he was almost asleep, Bois Sec saw the alligator in the form of a gigantic old lady with large gaping jaws filled with rows of brown teeth. The boy jerked fully awake and turned his attention to the real world around him.

He watched the soft tangle on both sides of the boat. Sometimes it closed in until it seemed there wasn't enough space to squeeze through. But BoBo knew the exact place to steer. The foliage always opened for him. Many times it appeared that he was neglecting the most obvious channel for a dead end, but he was always right in his choice.

The bayou channel began to widen bit by bit. The underbrush thinned until it was possible to see several yards past the bank. Soon the ground beside the stream was solid enough to support scattered bayou shanties. Bois Sec knew the next stop was not far away. He went back to the cabin to fetch the horn so BoBo could start heralding their approach to the settlement.

Bois Sec tried to blow the horn before taking it to BoBo. He sounded a sickly whining bray that tapered off to a splutter.

BoBo turned around, surprised. "Hey, you sound like a cow I had once. Thought she was a jackass, she did. Practiced braying every day . . ."

BoBo chuckled and gave Bois Sec the poling stick. He picked up the horn to give out the familiar two-tone summons.

Bois Sec watched him, trying to fathom the mystery of the full depth of the low sound and the piercing overtones of the high note. BoBo read his mind.

"First you pull your lips pretty tight from the corners and kind of stiffen them up from top and bottom. Then put the horn up and blow as hard as you can all the way from down in the belly. When you get ready for the high note, just keep on blowing but tighten the lips a little from the corners and it comes out by itself. Keep practicing and it won't be too long till you're able to do it as good as anybody."

He gave the signal again. By the time they were tied up alongside the rickety dock, the first customers of the day were waiting to come aboard.

BoBo was everywhere at once — making sales, bouncing around, talking. The women had never found him so agreeable or so easy to talk into a favorable trade. Everyone knew of his *joie de vivre,* but they also knew of his reputation for being a shrewd trader. Rumor flourished: Was he drinking during trading time? No, not enough to show. Did he have *le chere?* No, he would have mentioned her name or let some detail slip. Had he won big in a card game or horse race? No, word would have gotten there before him. No one asked him directly. That would have been an invasion of privacy. But it was okay to ask *all around* the question that was really on their minds.

"You have pretty good work coming up on the bayou, *ahn?*"

"Them shrimpers leaving lil extry money in Morgan City, *ahn?*"

"I hear some people downriver been runnin' pretty good mus'rat lines, *ahn?*"

"Prettier girls been showing up every year at them *fais-do-dos* over Bayou Lafourche, *ahn?*"

BoBo smiled and answered all the questions. They had no way of knowing that his excitement wasn't related to any of these things. He was caught up in the prospect of a new adventure. Bois Sec felt the same, but he did not show it as much as his *nonc.*

Mam Bergeron gathered several remnants of cloth with a few bright trimmings.

"Oh, you setting out to do a little sewing? Here, let Bois Sec refill your cup while we find some thread," BoBo offered as he laid out a tray of thread spools. The color choices were heavily in favor of blue, white, black, and yellow nankeen. The trimming didn't always match the material. The material was heavy and practical while the trimmings were very decorative. The ordinary bayou woman could not afford to buy separate clothes for special occasions, so she bought trimmings that would be worn until they were threadbare.

Mam Bergeron carefully examined and re-examined the spools of thread while she sipped her coffee. "You got some pretty paper do-dads?" she asked.

BoBo pulled some small rolls of colored tissue paper from under a shelf. "*Ahn!* You got a girl ready to jump the broom already?" he said, smiling. He knew that real flowers were available but it was customary to use homemade paper flowers for weddings. All the women related to the bride would spend weeks in advance making paper bouquets, flower chains, and decorative pieces for clothing and place settings. Paper flowers made better keepsakes than real ones.

She answered, "It's that girl Marie and that Abadie boy, Theo. They got moon eyes for each other. The priest be stopping by next week — we have ever thing ready by then. You know, we got a little *fais-do-do* this night. Why don't you and the boy come on over and spend a piece of the night? It's at the Abadie place. They cleaned out the whole barn and we all got together and laid a wood floor over the main place where the dancing's goin' on. You know you're sure welcome, and we wouldn't mind at all if you wanna bring 'long your squeeze box and make a tune or two. Who know, mebe you meet a nice widow and do some broom-jumping yourself."

People who knew seldom brought up a subject

that would revive memories of BoBo's marriage so many years ago. The marriage had ended when his young bride drowned in the muddy bayou waters. If BoBo had not brought in an outsider, it would never have happened. That is what everybody thought, but no one said so to BoBo.

The Babins and Bergerons had known each other for generations. They considered themselves *voisons,* neighbors. But it went deeper. They were closer than friends but not as close as relatives. BoBo and Bois Sec had many *voisons* on the bayou. He seemed not to notice Mam Bergeron's statement about his marital status.

"Why, Amy Bergeron, you know all the muscle in Louisiana couldn't hold me back from a good *fais-do-do*. You know I'll be first there and last gone." They both laughed. "Here you be gettin' all the cloth and I'll be throwing in the paper for lagniappe," he said, reverting to the business at hand.

The women left early enough that Bois Sec did not have to put on a second pot of coffee. The men would not be coming in tonight. Everyone would be at the festivities over at the Abadies'.

Bois Sec put on his new denims and a clean homespun nankeen shirt. They still had the smell of newly spun cloth that had not been exposed to dirt, sweat, and repeated washings in the strong lye soap. He tried to bring his unruly hair under control, but it was not used to the taming efforts of a comb. It insisted on going its own way.

BoBo wore his corduroy pants, new shirt, and a red silk scarf. He had a wide leather belt with a polished silver buckle and boots shined like new. He shaved his chin and waxed his mustache. By mixing a trace of soot from the lamp with the wax he was able to hide the gray reflections on his temples and mustache. He wasn't turning gray fast, but under bright light there appeared more highlights than he had noticed in earlier years.

The pair left the boat early so they would have time to visit along the way.

The community along the banks was like the last stop and the one before that, with only a few details changed. The villages along the bayous in the swampland were similar.

BoBo and Bois Sec called and waved at everyone they passed. Every so often they would stop for a cup of coffee and talk. From the kitchens came rich spice smells blended with the odor of pastry baked in an open oven.

BoBo was known as an expert judge of fine food because of his wide experience as a traveling man. His opinion about food was sought after because the cook was always sure of a compliment. He had many adjectives on hand so that even if he was not pleased with the food he could leave the cook feeling complimented.

After taking samples at several stops, BoBo and Bois Sec had managed to eat as much as a large meal before they reached the Abadie barn.

Chapter 6

The *Fais-do-do*

Several buggies and horses were already tied up outside the barn. The Broussards arrived in their buggy. On a buggy built for four they had packed twelve people. Every adult had one or two young ones on his lap. The twins were riding the horse and one was hanging on the luggage rack behind. Their arrival didn't seem unusual. Large families were common among the French Catholics. Most of the buggies, wagons, skiffs or pirogues were fully loaded.

In the barn, lanterns hung from high beams and candles were placed in buckets of sand around the edge of the floor.

The crowd gathered in small, scattered groups. The men talked about crops and hunting. The old folks watched the younguns over to one side while the women prepared the long table near the wall. It was loaded with goodies from every family there.

Kids were everywhere, running, playing chase and hide and seek. A few of the bolder ones would slip up to the table and try to sneak goodies. They had to be ready to dodge a tap on the head from a ladle held by the nearest *maman*. It was all done in good-natured fun.

The bandstand became the center of attention when the musicians began tuning and warming up their instruments. It seemed as though everyone was playing a different tune at first, but in a matter of seconds they'd settle on the same tune and they were off. After that they were guided by whomever could shout loudest to call the name of the next tune. In a crowd so large there were plenty of extra musicians and all would have their chance to play as one or another left the stand to *fais-do-do* on the floor.

There was seldom so much as a pause between tunes, except for special numbers such as "woman's choice," "change partners," and "fox chase the rabbit" and others that needed a special lineup of the dancers. Almost everybody enjoyed these special numbers — the boy who was too shy to ask that special girl; the older people who would normally use the excuse of old age to stay on the sidelines; the fathers who wanted to dance with their daughters for a few moments.

BoBo divided his time between the bandstand and the dance floor. He seemed to be all over the place. His red scarf would show at one end of the floor, and before it seemed possible that same flash of red would appear at the opposite end. He would flirt with everyone's girl, but no one took offense. On the bandstand he put on quite a show. He could call a dance, liven things up with a joke, or bring the group to laughter or tears with his songs. He could be the center of attention or he could disappear from the crowd.

Bois Sec did not move with such ease. He had the words to say, but they often came out at the wrong time. He did not feel like going outside and playing chase with the kids as he used to do at *fais-do-dos,* but he felt self-conscious about going out on the dance floor with the older group. All his friends seemed younger than before. He surely couldn't go over to the side where the *grandmeres* and *grand-peres* stood around the *bebes* on their pallets and in their cribs and boxes. There was no place on the floor where he could feel comfortable.

He wandered over behind the bandstand and tried to see a girl who had caught his eye before, but one of the older girls saw him and giggled. He felt out of place there too. The last place he had seen the girl was by the refreshment table, so he eased over in that direction. He walked the length of the table, first in one direction then the other, pretending to study the food.

A voice came from directly behind him. "My name is Minette. I'll bet you're Bois Sec."

He turned around slowly. The object of his search was addressing him from not more than a foot away. Her presence seemed to surround him, leaving him powerless to move or speak. He knew he had to say something or she would think he wasn't interested and go away. At last he found words, but he knew they were not the ones he wished to say.

"Tha's me. How come you know me and I don't know you?"

"Oh, I seen you and BoBo ever time you come round but you always too busy helping on the boat or playing silly games to see me." She didn't plan to let him off easy.

"*Nonc* BoBo keeps me pretty busy, but it sure looks like I'd remember you. You musta growed up some since I seen you 'cause I don't too often disremember a face." Her expression told him he had guessed the reason for not recognizing her. Quickly he sorted through his memory to find her face belonging to a scrawny, spindly-legged, scraggly-haired little pest who was always there whenever he and BoBo landed.

She continued to tease him. "You must be about the hungriest person around. I never seen anyone with a plate so piled up with food. You got enough there for three or four people. Mam Bergeron was sure trying to fatten you up for sure. Get another glass of punch and I'll have a bite with you, if you don't mind sharing."

Bois Sec knew then that this was a little kitten he could get along with. They went outside and sat on a bench to get acquainted and finish the plate of food.

In the shadows he could sense her eyes on him. Without the bright lights and surrounding audience he returned her gaze without embarrassment. She said, "I wish I could travel everywhere like you and BoBo. It seems all I ever see is Beaux Crois, the same houses and the same people and nothing exciting."

Bois Sec thought that anywhere Minette was would be exciting, but he said, "It ain't all fun and

71

excitement. But I like it better than I think I'd like staying in one place all the time unless I had somebody special to stay there for. I like meeting all the people and all, but I especially like the other side of traveling, too, when you're way off by yourself. You wouldn't believe how pretty everything is back where nobody goes. The animals just move around natural like without any fear of people. I wish you could see it."

She interrupted, "Oh, I wish I could go with you sometime and we could see it together. Things is so much better when you enjoy them with somebody you like."

She reached over and squeezed his hand. The warmth and softness spread from his hand to the rest of his body until he felt all mushy inside.

"We'll be gone a little extry long to do what we've got to do on this trip, but this is the first place I'm coming when we get through," he promised.

"When people like us make promises they usually leaves a token of that promise to remind theirselves when they're apart," she said. She seemed much more experienced in such matters than Bois Sec. He didn't like to reveal his ignorance, but he had to find out what it was all about.

"I'd like to leave a token . . . in fact, I'll give you anything I got that you'd like to have . . . but I don't know what a token is," he confessed.

"I'm glad you don't. That means you ain't never given a token to any other girl. A token ain't really anything that's worth anything except to them who gets it. It's just a little something that's all yours that when you gives it makes the other person think about you, like you had a little of that person with you all the time. It's what you might call a symbol. It's not what the thing is, it's what it stands for."

She reached up to her throat and pulled a hand-carved wooden button from her dress, handed it to Bois Sec, and said, "You see, this ain't much, but it's something you can carry with you all the time and it's all mine. I carved it myself and polished it. Hold it in your hand every day and I'll hold your token and it'll be like we were really together."

He fumbled in his pocket to give her something in return. His hand touched his knife first. That would be symbolic in a way, but he rejected it because the knife was also a symbol of sharpness and harshness that was so different from the soft Minette. Then his hand closed on the little puzzle that ol' Gaffe had given him earlier. The right words to say with the presentation occurred to him as he handed it to her.

"This little thing ain't much, it ain't near as pretty as the button you give me, but it says something about the way I feel. Just like the washer is on the stick and won't come off — they're bound to be together from now on, that washer and that stick — that's the way I want to be with you." Bois Sec figured that was just about the most profound thing he had ever said.

"Oh, Bois Sec, that's just about the sweetest thing I ever heard anybody say. All I give you was a old button and you give me something that was really and truly a symbol. You know what you're supposed to do after you exchange tokens, don't you?"

He gave her a puzzled look.

She answered in a tone of mock exasperation, "Oh, you ninny, you're supposed to seal it with a kiss!"

She grabbed him and gave him a kiss full on the lips before he realized what was happening. There was nothing in his past that could have prepared him for the emotion that exploded inside him. At that moment the world revolved around Minette.

At the conclusion of the brief kiss she pulled away from him, then she was gone.

Bois Sec couldn't bring himself to go back inside. He returned to the houseboat, glad to be alone.

Sometime later he was vaguely aware of flashes of light through his closed eyelids. Low rumbles and occasional crashes of sound told his unconscious that it was only a thunderstorm. The accompanying winds rocked the craft with a gentle soothing movement, and Bois Sec never fully awoke.

He didn't even know when BoBo returned.

Chapter 7

Maman Guidry

Bois Sec awoke to the sound of a steady, heavy rain. He looked over to see BoBo still curled up in his blanket, breathing in the deep even rhythm of one sound asleep. It was later than they usually arose, but the pounding rain and BoBo's sound sleep told him there was no hurry this morning. So, without moving a muscle except his eyelids, he let the rain soothe him back to sleep.

When he awoke again it was still raining, though not as heavy. He could hear the sounds of cooking utensils rattling and smell the rich aroma of boiling coffee and eggs with bacon.

"Hey, sleepy head. It's about time to start some action around here," BoBo spoke over the cooking sounds.

"I notice you seems to stir up a lil action here and there. How come you gets off so easy makin' light with all them other fellers' pretty girls?" BoBo smiled at Bois Sec's question.

"Speaking of other fellers' pretty girls, a right pretty lil thing asked me to give this note to someone she musta thought was pretty special," he said, and handed Bois Sec a folded piece of paper.

Bois Sec eagerly took the paper from BoBo and opened it without speaking. He read the brief note written in dainty feminine hand:

> Don't forget what we talked about. I'll think about you ever day forever —
>
> Love
> XXXX
> Minette

He read the note several times. He felt more elation with each reading. Finally, he spoke. "BoBo, how do you feel when you're really in love?"

BoBo chose to change the subject. Some things a youngster would have to learn on his own. "Let's take a bite of breakfast while it's hot. There ain't no hurry to be off till this rain lets up. Ain't likely to be anybody around, so I think I'll have another study of that map. Mebe we can figure something out."

They enjoyed a quiet breakfast with each lost in his own thoughts.

As soon as they finished, BoBo left Bois Sec to take care of the cleaning chores and spread the map out for further study.

The boy said, "I swear you're goin' to stare a hole through that paper if you keep looking so hard."

Bois Sec's uneasy feeling about the map returned. Again he had the feeling that the map held some of the evil of those in the past who had handled it. He thought of those forces said to hover near the ominous "X" scrawled by a blood-stained hand so many years ago. For BoBo the treasure at the point shown by the crude "X" on the map had become a symbol of that secret fear he held of the unknown. He had told himself many times that such fears of the unknown had no foundation, but he was not convinced.

"I think I'm beginning to get a little sense out of these chicken scratchin's. I can get in purty close to it, but I'm goin' to have to have a lil help finding just exactly where it is we're goin'. I think we keep goin' south and get rid of this load and then go digging. We beginning to look like Noah's ark."

He was referring to the increasing stock of live produce they had taken on board in trade. Several crates of chickens and a pig were on the stern of the small vessel. BoBo had accepted the pig in trade only because it was near the last stop before reaching Morgan City. Bundles of furs were piling up inside, crowding the already cramped space.

On another scrap of paper and on the margins of the map, BoBo was studiously making notes in his cramped writing style. He continued bent over the work for more than an hour until the rain had slowed to a drizzle. He then rose, put on his yellow slicker, and started the ritual of getting under way. He didn't need the rain gear for long. The sun soon replaced the clouds and turned the remaining moisture into a low-hanging, steamy tropical fog.

For some hours the floating store wound through

twisting, bending, overgrown bayou waters to finally emerge into the deep, steady flowing Atchafalaya River. There, strong currents made the push pole unnecessary.

BoBo used a long oar on the stern to guide the boat to their port in Morgan City before nightfall. He paddled the craft into a slip between two shrimp boats and secured for the night. BoBo usually took advantage of a stopover in Morgan City to go out on the town, but on this night he lit the lantern, unfolded the map, and was shortly hard at work studying and making notes on the ancient parchment. Bois Sec snuggled down into his moss-filled mattress and soon had mixed dreams of the scary old woman and the soft, beautiful Minette.

The night was well used when the light was extinguished and BoBo settled down for some rest.

The first rays of sunlight over Morgan City found BoBo and Bois Sec dressed and ready to go into town. Bois Sec filled the small coffee pot with fresh water and was putting dark roasted coffee beans into the grinder when BoBo stopped him.

"Hey, hold on there. We gonna let somebody else do the cooking this morning. *Maman* Guidry down to the cafe make the best coffee with eggs and ham in the Atchafalaya Basin. That ain't to say our cooking ain't good, but sometime it get so everybody's cookin' tastes better'n what you get used to day after day. Throw a lil feed out to the critters so they look fat and satisfied when we get to the market."

Bois Sec answered, "That sound like one good idea. You sure don't hurt my feelings none wanting a change. It won't take me half a minute to throw out the feed."

They walked down the deeply rutted narrow shell road in front of a long row of high-roofed buildings fronting on the river. Soon they approached a huge, freshly painted white frame building with swinging doors and a long row of windows across the front. A hand-carved sign over the door read: MAMAN GUIDRY'S KITCHEN.

They entered and found a place at one of several large wooden tables covered with bright red and white checked tablecloths. The large, airy room was saturated with the odor of food cooking on the stove. Faint reminders of previous meals also lingered in the air. The effect was rich, delicious, and appetizing.

A shriek came from the kitchen. "*Sacre!* Hey! BoBo Babin, you ol' son a na gun, where you been? I ain't seen you in a coon's age!"

A large woman with arms outstretched half ran, half bounced from the kitchen toward their table. BoBo leaped to his feet to grab the mountain of juggling flesh in his arms. "*Maman,* big *Maman* Guidry! I see you been eatin' your own cookin' again. I gonna have to grow another set of arms to reach around you!"

Maman Guidry laughed and replied, "You two getting skinny as snakes! You gonna have to stay around a few days and let ol' *Maman* put a lil fat on them bones. I bet you ain't eat a good meal in a week. You men folk out batching on that boat alla time don't know how to take care of yourselves. BoBo, why don't you get a good woman to take care of you

80

and that youngun? Enough of this jawing — lemme get something on the stove for you."

"Now, don't you go to nothing special for us. Scramble up a couple of eggs with some ham on the side. We gotta get on up the road and get done the tradin'."

She ignored his protests against special treatment and went on to pour two steaming half cups of thick black coffee. She finished filling one of the cups with warm milk thick with cream and sweetened it with a large tablespoon of sugar. She added a small shot of whiskey to the other cup.

While they sipped *Maman* Guidry's special blend of coffee she disappeared into the kitchen.

"That fat *maman* sure make a fine cup of coffee," BoBo commented.

Bois Sec was used to drinking straight black coffee on the boat with BoBo. *Maman* Guidry was the only person he knew who could make a really good cup of coffee *au lait*. He was convinced that she required a body of great size to contain her great heart.

She returned shortly with two large plates loaded with eggs, sausage, ham, bacon, grits, strawberry preserves, and a pile of biscuits on the side. She left the plates and went back to refill the coffee cups. She busied herself with other customers while they ate and then joined them with fresh coffee refills and hot sweet rolls.

"Now you boys looks like you ready to face the day," she said. "You can't get nothing done on an empty stomach."

BoBo replied, "You fixed us up for sure. I'm so full now I can't get up. *Maman,* you gotta be the best cook anywhere." She smiled and a touch of red colored her cheeks while he continued. *"Maman,* I gotta lil problem. We trying to find a place called Pont Diable down across from Gran Terre. You been around a long time, and you usta live down in that direction. You ever hear of a place like that?"

The smile left her face when she answered, "BoBo, BoBo, don't you go tell me you went and find one of them treasure maps?"

He paled and tried to silence her. *"Shh, Maman,* don't say things like that so loud. Mighta knowed there's no puttin' a thing over on *Maman* Guidry. I think this time we got the real thing, but we ain't too anxious to have no more'n we have to in on it."

The big woman shook her head slowly and replied, this time in a soft voice, "I sure ain't too happy about you getting the bug. I seen it do bad things to too many people. Seems like when a man gets that on the mind that's all he can think of. You got everything you need — but I mighta knowed, you being a traveling man without roots, that sooner or later it got to happen. I don't know whether I should help you or not, but you know I can't turn down ol' BoBo. Mebe it's just as well you have a fling at it and get it outta the system.

"I can't help you a whole lot, but I have heard of the place. One of the ol' folk down there know a lot more'n I do. I just know what I heard when I'se a youngun. Ain't too many folk left old enough to know firsthand about the place. I tell you some things I heard, then you decide if you're still interested." She paused and grew more serious.

"Pont Diable is one bad place. Somebodies say it ain't no accident how it got that name. They say the devil found the evilest place in the world down in the swamp where nobody can ever go, and there he built a gate that open straight to hell. They say when some of the evil spirits gets too cantankerous to sta y in hell, the devil sends them up to Pont Diable until they straighten out. I know ain't nobody used to go fishin' or chasin' hounds down that way.

"The whole place got tore up and changed around in the big wind back in 1856. That's almost forty years ago. You'd have to find somebody 'round before then that could tell you anything. Just about everybody out on the islands and most of the people close to the beach got blowed away or drowned. A lot of them folks still alive at the end of the blow got up and left, the Guidrys included. I was just a youngun then. New folks has moved back since. They planted a bunch of oak trees all up and down Grand Isle to keep the whole thing from blowin' away. People out on Gran Terre either forgot or never knew about the big wind."

She finally reached the point in her story that would be most helpful. "They's one ol' man I know personal who didna get blowed away or scared away. He lived through the plague when Bronze John killed nearly everbody in New Orleans before he came south to stay. He wasn't no real young man then, but last I heard he's still alive and doin' pretty good. After coming through Bronze John and the blow one right after the other, he got convinced that there ain't no way he could have lived without he had some special powers. Everybody around him got killed. He set hisself up as a *remède* man after that, and a lot of people say he's got a way with the swamp

83

spirits. People come from all over with their ailments and when they thinks they're hexed or when they needs *gri gri* that only a *remède* man can give. He knew the old names of all the places and what was where before the wind.

"This old man, they call him Amos Boudreaux, he the onliest man I know anywhere that knows the swamps and was here before and after the big hurricane. They's bound to be others, of course, but I doubt they'd be able to help you like old Amos. You'd wind up having to see a *remède* man anyway, goin' in where all them swamp spirits abide." She paused, smiled, and winked at BoBo. "You gonna bring big *Maman* back just a lil flour sack full a dem gold pieces?"

She knew that BoBo had a healthy respect for things of the swamp that he didn't understand. He would surely be discouraged from pursuing the matter further after her story. She was mistaken. Not even *Maman* Guidry, who knew BoBo as well as anyone he visited on his rounds up and down the bayou, knew of his secret desire to win over the swamp spirits, nor could she know that Bois Sec was now inspired by *le jeune file* with the dark hair and flashing eyes.

"You know it, *Maman,* I bring you back a tote sack full. You just point me in the right direction to find old man Amos Boudreaux, as you call him."

"*Bon ami, cher,* these are no laughing things I tell you. I tell you just the way I was told. The stories are old and should not be taken lightly." It was apparent that whether or not the stories were true, she believed them.

BoBo was very much concerned, and his old fears gnawed inside him. But his determination was stronger than his fear. He would carry on with the project in spite of anything anyone said — but he would take every possible measure to protect himself and Bois Sec against the unseen forces in the swamp.

BoBo saw her concern and answered, "If that *remède* man is as good as people say, he should be able to fix us up. I ain't really makin' light of nothin'. But where there's so much at stake, I guess a man's got to expect to take a lil risk. We have our minds set to go through with the thing now that we've started, and I guess we're pretty much bound to finish it up or die trying. Bois Sec and me, we been through some pretty good times and some pretty rough times, and we always come out with our necks in one piece. This boy got enough spunk to handle just about anything I can. I know they's a man named Amos Boudreaux that's got the answer. It may take a lil longer, but you know we're gonna wind up doin' some digging."

"BoBo, I don't mind telling you I'd sure like to disencourage you, but I'll help you all I can. You know that. You know, too, that if all this wild goose chasing does turn up something you don't owe me for nothing. Here's what you do. You go over to west of Barataria Bay to a place called Galliano, then just about a mile or so northeast toward Little Lake lives ol' Amos in a big ol' cypress house in a thicket out in the middle of a marsh. You can get there by way of Black Cat Bayou. Here, I better make a map for as far as I can remember from Galliano."

She took a clean white napkin and bent into a

cramped position to start the crude diagram for BoBo. She explained where the main landmarks were as she drew.

BoBo said, "We need to get the houseboat down there if we're gonna haul anything out. Inland it would be about eighty or a hundred mile of marsh and swamp bayou that I don't know too good. I gotta go on the Atchafalaya all the way back to the big river, then I cut off back down Bayou LaFourche to go right by Galliano. That would be over a hundred miles. I think we better try to buoy up the boat for a heavy load." He was thinking aloud.

Maman Guidry broke in. "I been through that short route, but you gotta do a lot more than just go through once or twice to know the bayous. I couldn't begin to help you there. I know they ain't no talking you out of it now, so I just wish you the best. Be sure to take care of yourself and that youngun and get back here in one piece. That's all I want you to bring me back. You're one of the best swamp men I know. I guess if anybody can make it, you will." She gave him a hug and a wet kiss on the cheek, then gave Bois Sec a kiss on the forehead.

"Bois Sec, you growin' like a weed! I wish you'd stay here with me while BoBo goes off on this madness, but I can see the fire in your eyes. Don't you go reaching in that pocket — your money's no good in *Maman* Guidry's. Get on out of here! And when you come back I hope you got a boat load of goodies or else you got all this nonsense out of the system. God bless. Now, get yourselves gone."

Chapter 8

The Produce House

The produce house was a large, high-ceilinged, rambling building with open beams and raw, un-painted plank walls. Everywhere there was activity, and smells found no other place: the musky smells of stacked furs, the warm sickly sweet smell of fresh blood from the long slaughter racks in back, the smell of wet feathers, the fresh and not-so-fresh ma-nure smells, the dairy smells of cheese and sour cream, the crisp smells of new vegetables and fruit, the sharp smells hinting of shrimp, catfish, salt and rotting junkfish carried in from the waterfront breezes. The full mixture of smells sharpened to the senses. The sounds of clanking milk cans, the cack-ling, clucking, grunting, squealing animal sounds, the rough men's language, and the general confusion and activity gave the whole area of the produce house a special overpowering feel. It was unique.

BoBo took the surroundings for granted as he

talked about prices and trades and exchanged gossip. Bois Sec was fascinated by the whole thing every time he went there with BoBo. It was all part of the grown-up world that he was so anxious to grow into on the one hand but that he feared on the other.

There was much he did not understand about a man's world. There were things a man had to do. He had to stand up to another man if his rights were challenged. He had to help another person who needed help. He could accept gifts or help from another, but he could not take advantage of another's generosity. To take charity was to be shamed. He had to be hard. There was little room for softness in the swamp. He had to kill to provide meat for the table, whether it was wild game or a tame chicken. If a favorite pet dog became an egg sucker, that dog had to be destroyed because he threatened the livelihood of the family. There were adjustments a boy had to make to become a man if he were to survive.

A boy had to be prepared to take his place as a man when the time came. If he didn't he had to be prepared to face ridicule and scorn and finally be forced to the outside world. Apparently, weaknesses could be tolerated there.

There were some parts of growing up that Bois Sec had to accept because he was of the swamp. He loved the swamp and the people with their deep down *joie de vivre,* but sometimes the harsher realities disturbed him.

In the produce house he found the long slaughter room hard to accept. He could thrill to the hunt of wild game and look forward to fresh meat on the table. He could wring a chicken's neck or watch the butchering of a single pig or yearling without a second thought, but the mass slaughter of unsuspecting animals bothered him. He could stand alongside the men and appear not to be bothered by the drama of death taking place a few feet away, but inside he wanted to run away.

Bois Sec could not avoid seeing certain human qualities in all living creatures. He saw even the dumbest creatures as beings that had feelings and emotions.

Bois Sec knew there had to be places like the slaughter room, but he hoped that on this visit he would not have to enter the large rear room of the building, especially so soon after the recent feast at *Maman* Guidry's.

They were in luck. A large red-faced man wearing a dirty white shirt and a leather bow tie was gesturing with a well-chewed cigar toward a group of homespun clad men standing around him.

BoBo called, "Hey, Patte-Rouge, you ol' chicken stealing, horse trading, sonana gun! Here's ol' BoBo in town again to get his bones picked by a double-dealin' produce man."

"*Ahn,* BoBo, the prices you talk me into givin' for the scrawny chickens and spoiled eggs and shedding hides you bring in from the swamp put me out of business. You're lucky I be such a charitable person. What kinda trash you gonna try to stick poor ol' Patte-Rouge with this time?"

They were exchanging the rough humor of outdoor men. This was their way of giving greetings without appearing soft. BoBo knew Patte-Rouge paid as much as he could afford and still clear a fair profit. Patte-Rouge in turn knew that anything brought in by BoBo would be well cared for and of good quality. If BoBo knew a fur had been cut in the wrong place in the skinning, he would make the fact known. They had traded for many years. Each tried to better the other in insults as a cover for a deep friendship that both were too embarrassed to express openly.

BoBo answered, "I got a pretty good load. I'm gonna have to borrow a hand cart and take three or four loads to get it all down here. I got a special good load of rat hides except for one lil bundle I get from the young Abadie boy. You might be able to piece some of them, otherwise I threw them in for a good cup coffee. I don't know about that boy. I try to tell him to cut the hide just at the joints and cross the bottom then reach the hands up inside to loosen and pull it off but he always uses the knife inside the hide to get it loose and he get a few nicks. I guess he's afraid to get the hands dirty or something. His *papa* always bring enough good furs to more'n make up the difference though."

Patte-Rouge gestured with his cigar toward a cart standing in the far corner of the large main room near an enormous stack of empty chicken crates. "There's the cart . . . Help yourself. You need someone to help with the loading?"

"No, thanks. Bois Sec and me need the exercise to work off *Maman* Guidry's breakfast."

"It's a wonder you can walk after her stuffin'," Patte-Rouge laughed. "I'll see you in the office with the coffee as soon as you get the loading done."

They went over to get the rickety two-wheel pull

cart. BoBo said, "Bois Sec, put them two side boards on and we won't have to make so many trips."

Bois Sec picked up the two side boards that were leaning against the wall and placed them one at a time into slots on either side of the shallow bed. The wheels squeaked on ungreased axles and the loose boards rattled as BoBo pulled and Bois Sec pushed the cart over the rough oyster shell-covered road. A few people looked up to note the cause of the disturbance, then turned back to their business.

The two loaded as many crates as the cart would comfortably hold, then stacked on one more. They lashed the unwieldy cargo down with a length of line and started their return. The squeaks and rattles turned to creaks and groans as they forced the overloaded vehicle back to the produce house. They had to make three loads for the live produce and another for the furs. Each trip seemed to be the last the old cart could make without breaking down, but after the last load it was none the worse for wear.

They met in Patte-Rouge's office to talk terms over strong black coffee. Patte-Rouge poured Bois Sec an undiluted cup with the adults. It made him feel good to be included, even if the coffee was pretty bad. It had the taste of having been boiled several times until it was almost as thick as sorghum molasses. The thick, bitter liquid would have tasted better diluted with anything. But Bois Sec was still glad his host had not offered something weaker.

They put on a show of haggling over prices, with each pretending the other had gotten the better of the deal. Bois Sec could tell from BoBo's expression that he had received more than he expected in the deal, but he was always one to try for a little extra.

"Patte-Rouge, you ol' mule-skinner, you getting harder to deal with every trip. Why don't you throw in that stack of empty barrels outside there? You need to get them out of your way. They just junking up the place more'n it is."

"Why you need them barrels for? I can't tell when I might need them to haul out something. A empty barrel's always a good thing to have around to pack things in."

BoBo answered, "You got mebe a dozen or so out here. I don't need but six or eight. I gonna go in dry dock a day or two. I wanted to tar up some barrels and rig 'em so's to buoy up for a lil heavier load."

"You know I just carrying you on, BoBo. Take all you need. I'll be glad to get shut of them. You can even use the cart to haul them out if you want to. You ain't goin' off somewhere to stay, are you? Anything else I can do, you just got to ask."

BoBo said, "I'd be much obliged for the barrels — and since you mention it, they might be a lil something you can do if it won't put you out too much. I don't figure my business is gonna take too long. I'll be hauling something back and I'll probably be coming by river since there ain't no dry dock to replace the buoys on Grand Isle. It'll be at least two or three weeks, but it could be a lot longer depending on how things go. What I need is a place to store my goods and everything loose on board while we're gone. We need to lighten up some and get a lil more space. An' say, *bon ami,* I much appreciate it if you don't say too much about this. If anyone ax, just say we be back by and by."

Patte-Rouge was anxious to help in any way he could. He wondered if BoBo was in some kind of trouble.

"We get you fixed up fine. You better let me help you else the whole town's likely to find out what's goin on. You can count on ol' Patte-Rouge to not let the word out." He shoved aside some of the clutter of paper on his desk and moved closer to BoBo. Now he spoke in a low voice. "We'll stash your gear in the loft over the office here and box it up so's nobody will know what we got. I got some extry tarp we can throw on top of the cart while we're moving and nobody will know you ain't just bringing in more produce ashore. We wait till just after dark.

"I got the use of a lil dry dock down the channel that about everybody's forgot about because it's so growed over. We'll have to brace up one of the beams that's rotted out, but that won't be too hard with the three of us workin'. I'll get some new block and tackle from the slaughter room and you can raise the boat and rig it up where there won't be too many to take notice. You got a big part of the day left here. So far as anybody else is concerned, I'm gonna hire you to tar up some barrels for me. I know it'll be out of character for you to do a regular day's work for pay, but mebe people'll just think you're tryin' to raise a lil extry for boat repairs or something."

Patte-Rouge was caught up in the idea of helping BoBo prepare for his mysterious mission. He hoped BoBo would loosen up and give a hint about

what he was up to, but he had no intention of prying further.

He turned to look at the boy. "Bois Sec, go roll the best of them barrels around to the shed in back and me and BoBo will carry one of the iron pots back for cooking the tar."

The job was hot and messy. They had to tack the tops on to the barrels securely then swab the hot, sticky tar over all the cracks with the remains of a worn-out mop. After each barrel was sealed, water was splashed on the dry wood to seal it to further tightness.

By nightfall they were both ready to return to the boat for some rest, but Patte-Rouge would have none of that. He insisted that they get the extra gear stashed early, else they would attract too much attention working into the night. It took several loads, but at last they finished unloading.

On the return trips they took the sealed barrels, the assortment of blocks and tackle, and other materials needed to repair the dry dock and rig the buoys. They untied the boat and Patte-Rouge guided them down an overgrown, apparently little used channel to a secluded slip hidden from view on the bank by a large clump of trees.

"Bois Sec, you can stay here and settle down to a little rest while I take Patte-Rouge back in the skiff. We got more'n a little bit of work to do tomorrow," BoBo suggested rather than ordered. The boy was happy to do his bidding. The day had been long and tiring.

BoBo took the big man back and stayed only

long enough to have a pair of social drinks before returning through the black channel to the boat. He didn't strike a light so as not to attract attention to their whereabouts. Only a few faint beams of moonlight filtered through the thick foliage overhead to cast flickers of silver reflections on the quiet water. Inside the quarters it was black as the tar they had used to seal the barrels. Soon he joined Bois Sec in deep sleep, serenaded by a million swamp creatures.

Chapter 9

Rigging the Houseboat

The sun had not risen when they were awakened by Patte-Rouge's husky voice booming through a cloud of cigar smoke. "Awaken, *mon amis*. If we gonna get this here boat outfitted we gotta get ourselves busy."

Bois Sec rubbed the sleep from his eyes and saw that Patte-Rouge was accompanied by two men. One was a tall, gangling man with pronounced hawk-like features, a long nose, deep-set sleepy eyes, thin lips under a heavy mustache, and a solemn expression. The other was short and thin with a round pixie face fringed with a red beard, a large ruddy nose, and protruding ears. His head appeared not to match his body. His face was set in a perpetual grin that revealed two missing front teeth.

Patte-Rouge explained, "I brought along a couple of trusted friends, Pierre the short and Alcee the tall, to make the work go faster. Don't worry your head a little bit. They knows how to keep the mouth shut for sure. It will without doubt be very warm to work the whole day, so I brought along a keg of beer to wet our throats when the sun gets high."

Bois Sec livened up the fire and started the coffee while BoBo threw several thick slices of bacon into the big black skillet. While the bacon sizzled and crackled and curled up in its grease, he cracked some eggs into an empty syrup bucket.

By the time the breakfast was finished and the second cup of coffee poured, the sun was just beginning to send a few golden flickers through the walls of leaves surrounding the small slip.

By late afternoon they had managed to raise the boat, attach the buoys, and lower it again to the water. Their success was largely due to the efforts of an entire ship's crew who had, among others, somehow gotten word of a party. All joined in the celebration. Sometime during the activities, more beer kegs and a few bottles were added to the original supply of refreshments.

The procession that made its way from the secret dry dock was a strange one. Even with the additional buoys, the deck of the houseboat was barely above water because of the crowd on board.

If anyone at that moment had suggested that the purpose of the expedition was to search for treasure he would not have been believed.

BoBo would be uneasy until the whole affair was over. He knew someone would be sure to follow as soon as they were out of sight.

He passed the remaining refreshments to a nearby skiff to be taken ashore, which had the effect of moving the center of the party. The remaining passengers on the houseboat soon left with the party.

BoBo and Bois Sec were finally alone.

"BoBo?"

"Yeah, kid, what's on the mind?"

"BoBo, I's just wonderin', you got that map put up good and safe?" Bois Sec could imagine one of the characters of the day sneaking aboard during the night to knife them during their sleep for the key to their quest.

BoBo laughed. His voice seemed to express no doubt when he replied, "Don't you worry your head. I got that map good and safe. Besides, nobody can get on this boat without me hearing."

Bois Sec was not comforted by that thought. He knew that BoBo sometimes slept more soundly than he imagined.

The worry faded, though, as they were lulled to sleep by the soft rocking of the boat and the sounds of revelry in the distant street. Tomorrow would be time enough to clean up the mess and litter left on the boat by the visitors of the day.

Chapter 10

In Galliano

BoBo found the marked main channel that soon turned into Bayou Lafourche. The irregular marsh areas and winding channels formed a maze of green and blue stretching as far as the eye could see. The marsh turned into swamp and slowed in on the waterway.

They tied up at a small private dock. On the shore about thirty yards from the water was a small, thatch-roofed hut on stilts. BoBo, followed closely by Bois Sec, walked toward the hut to get permission for tying up and to ask directions to Amos Boudreaux's place. They had almost reached the hut when from the shadows underneath appeared the biggest, blackest dog either had ever seen. He jumped between them and the shaky stairway leading up to the hut. He stood stiff-legged, growling and staring at them with small, ferocious eyes. The bristly hair on his back stood erect and his muscles quivered as though he was readying himself to tear the visitors apart.

A voice came from the top of the stairs, but neither BoBo nor Bois Sec looked toward it. Their attention was on the beast standing guard before them. "Don't worry about ol' Fideaux," they heard. "He hardly ever bites anybody that don't provoke him."

BoBo answered in a voice not so steady, "You just tell me what provokes him and I'll try to be extry careful not to give him cause to get aroused."

"He gets awful bothered by sudden movements and when somebody turns their back on him and ignores him. But the main thing that gets him upset is when somebody crosses his territory."

"I ain't plannin' no fast moves and you can be sure I ain't turnin' my back on him. Now you just tell me where his territory is and I'll give him plenty of room."

The voice answered, "It's hard to say where his territory is today. He likes to change it from time to time. Chances are you ain't in it now or he'd be chewing you up. That ol' dog is peculiar and set in his ways. I never seen anything like him, unless mebe it's a man what lives in the swamp a couple of miles or so from here. A crazy old man by the name of Amos Boudreaux."

"That happens to be one of the things I wanted to talk to you about. I wanted to tie up here for the night and go out to old Amos' place tomorrow. I was wondering if mebe you could give directions out to his place . . ." BoBo said, his attention still on the dog. He had yet to look at the owner of the voice at the top of the stairs.

The voice laughed and said, "I don't particular mind you tying up here as long as you like. But I wouldn't plan to go over to that old man's house early in the morning. He don't get moving around at all till about dinner time. If you go on over there tonight you'll get him just about the right time for that old man. *Ahn!* You wake the crazy old man, he'd chase you off and chances are he wouldn't let you get near his place again.

"They's people go out there all the time for curses and *gri gri*. They say there ain't no better *remède* maker. He's supposed to be pretty good at making and casting off spells, too, not that I put too much stock in that sort of thing. He's the oddest one I ever seen. Unless I had a pretty bad ailment and had tried everything else, I wouldn't go near that old coot at all. There's a lot of people that swears by him, say he got a way of fixin' things up — whatever it is might be wrong."

He proceeded to give them about the same directions that *Maman* Guidry had given them earlier, but the directions made more sense on location. She had left out some details that she had probably forgotten over the years. It was good that they had fresh instructions; otherwise they could have missed the route.

BoBo said, "I'm much obliged for the directions and the offer to tie up for the night. But I think we'll take your advice and try to get on out there before it gets dark."

The two backed slowly and carefully toward the dock and on to the boat, keeping their eyes on the dog, which continued to growl and threaten. They didn't turn around until they had reached the end of the dock. Even then they very slowly and deliberately eased the boat away from the dock. They did not relax until the boat was safely in the middle of the stream. Not once had either of them looked at the person who had spoken from the top of the stairs.

Chapter 11

The House in the Swamp

The water route to the old man's house was not far, but the winding, overgrown channel was tricky. A less experienced swamp man than BoBo would probably have lost his way. Bois Sec wondered if other strangers searching out the old man found him without a guide. Probably not, he concluded.

The old man's house was not visible at all from the bayou. A boat dock, badly in need of repair, was the only indication that they had reached their destination. Even that might have been overlooked had it not been marked by upright posts on either side with a sagging cross plank between showing "AMOS" in dripping, hand-painted letters. On the opposite side of the landing a watersoaked pirogue with the same "AMOS" lettered in fading red on the bow was pushing up through the mud near the bank. From the projecting bow they saw a large cottonmouth unwind and slither into the water near a supporting post.

The fading light under the deep foliage was turning the scene into black shadows with gray green highlights. An unlit rusted lantern hung from a peg on one of the uprights supporting the sign. After tying up, BoBo lifted the lantern from the peg to discover half the bottom was rusted through. It was useless, so he used the boat's lantern instead.

The narrow dock looked too rickety to support the weight of both man and boy. Neither wanted to wade through the moccasin-infested water. It was widely said but more widely disbelieved that the deadly snakes would not strike in water. Bois Sec had seen hundreds of the snakes without feeling afraid, but the snake at the landing had seemed as though it had been placed there as a warning.

BoBo went first, making his way step by shaky step. He kept to the edge of the quivering walkway where it was somewhat supported by partly rotted crossbeams. Barely past the point of no return, the creaking turned to cracking and BoBo sprinted cat-like to the bank. Bois Sec's heart was in his throat when BoBo turned to hold the lantern up to indicate that it was his turn. He knew that if he kept his *nonc's* confidence there could be no hesitation. He had scarcely taken three steps when the cracking sound started. He tried two more quick steps when the support snapped, almost throwing him into the water before it caught on a piece of broken piling.

Bois Sec froze. He felt the piling slowly sinking in the soft bottom. He could imagine the cottonmouth joined by scores of like creatures slithering and wriggling just beneath the surface of the black water.

"Easy lad . . . slow now. Get on your knees. That's it! Now get your hands down . . . okay, stretch out now, spread your weight out and edge this way. Slow, now, slow!" BoBo hoarsely whispered his instructions.

Bois Sec made his way bit by bit over the sagging platform barely inches above the snake-filled water. When BoBo saw he was fighting a losing struggle, he ripped one of the looser boards off the ramp and stretched it as far as he could toward Bois Sec. The sagging became worse, threatening to throw them both into the water. BoBo shoved the board forward so Bois Sec could reach it, then eased himself back to the bank as quickly as he could safely do so.

In a quiet but forceful voice he instructed the frightened boy, "Don't panic. Take the loose board . . . that's it. Put the end in the water and push yourself to the other side. Slow, now . . . don't move fast or the whole rotten thing will give way. Okay, now roll over and ease your way back to the boat. Slow, now. Grab the upright, it's pretty secure. Okay now, board the boat and go do what we should've done in the first place when we seen this rotten excuse for a dock. Get the skiff and row over."

Soon the two were making their way up the barely visible path. BoBo held the lantern high and beat the tall grass with a stick in advance of their feet. It had become quite dark during their incident on the dock. Night comes quickly in the swamp.

The two made enough disturbance to give unseen crawling creatures an opportunity to get out of the way. Several yards past the bank, the brush opened into a clearing of sorts with a large blocky silhouette just the other side. A single dim light was visible from the window of an upstairs corner room. It had a gloomy, unwelcome appearance.

Bois Sec said, "Them that says a lot of people come up here mebe got a little mixed up in what they calls a lot of people. Sure don't look to me like they've beat out much of a trail gettin' here. I wonder how many of them got started and never made it this far?"

BoBo answered, "It sure is strange, for a fact. If the old man's as strange as everything else around here, we're in for something, I'll guarantee. I think we shoulda done what we started to do in the first place and wait until morning to come out here. I'm beginning to wonder if people been telling us straight. If I hadn't heard about this man from *Maman* Guidry, I think I'd just as soon go out and try to find the place on our own."

They reached the foot of one of the large outside staircases that formed an inverted "V" under the gallery of the sprawling Creole house. The house was in good shape, in contrast to the dock. The railing felt solid as the trunk of an oak tree as they started the ascent to the raised gallery. The lantern reflected full red trimming on the cross beams and around the windows. The closed shutters were solid black. The second story was similarly painted and trimmed. Heavy double front doors were painted to match the shutters. A solid black, cast iron knocker almost blended with the background.

The metallic clank of the knocker seemed to echo through long tunnels from deep inside the house's hidden chambers. In the distant interior was the muffled sound of scraping furniture and the softer sound of padded feet moving toward the doors at which BoBo and Bois Sec waited. Bois Sec had a fleeting impulse to escape back down the stairs when he heard a doorknob rattle. The door swung slowly outward.

Chapter 12

Old Man
Amos Boudreaux

A stooped little old man shorter than Bois Sec stood before them. His snow white hair bushed out from his head like the mane of a lion. An equally white mustache hid his mouth and much of his receding chin. Small, watery eyes squinted over thick square lenses, attempting to focus on the intruders. His ancient but wrinkle-free face reflected a waxen yellow from the smoking lamp he held at a precarious angle in his thin hand. A once-white but now gray nightgown was draped over winter longjohns tucked into heavy woolen socks.

They stood staring at each other for more than a minute before BoBo broke the silence with, "How do you do?"

"What?"

"I said, how do you do?" BoBo said, this time louder and more distinct.

"I heerd what you said. You think because I'm old I'm getting deef? How do I do what?" the old man answered.

"Whatever it is you do."

"I'm talking to you right now."

"Are you Amos Boudreaux?"

"Some people calls me Amos and some people calls me Boudreaux. I even met a man once called me Mr. Boudreaux, but ain't nobody ever called me Amos Boudreaux."

"I guess that's close enough. We've come a long way to talk to you."

"You must be getting what you come for because that's just what you're doin', talking to me."

"I didn't want to talk with you about just anything. I wanted to talk about something special," said BoBo, getting annoyed.

"You ain't said nothing particularly special yet."

"Do you mind if we come in?"

"Come in where?"

"Where you are."

"Can't. I'm here."

"I mean in the house there where we can talk in private." BoBo was getting visibly annoyed. Bois Sec was confused with the whole conversation.

"I guess that's okay. I used to be a private once. That was a long time ago . . . had a friend then was a corporal."

He continued talking about his army experiences as he turned and walked slowly away down a wide dark corridor. He ignored BoBo and Bois Sec as he continued on his way, talking to himself and gesturing with the smoking lamp that threatened at any moment to spill its globe or flame or both.

BoBo ordinarily did not enter a house without an invitation, but he had come too far to be left standing at the door. He left the lantern beside the door and followed the strange little old man. Bois Sec was right behind.

The old man entered a tall, narrow door off the corridor and for a moment only the glow and a long, dancing shadow from the door reminded them that they were not alone. The door opened into a room so large that the light from the shaky lamp barely revealed the walls. The corners and moving shadows cast from massive furniture remained black.

The weird procession filed into a smaller side room. The old man placed the lamp on the corner of a very large, cluttered desk and sat down in a straight, high-backed chair, which had the effect of making him appear even shorter. Scarcely more than his head and shoulders showed above the desk.

He surveyed his guests over the thick lenses for several moments before speaking. "Since you're here you may as well have a cup of something hot."

He motioned BoBo toward the simmering pot on a small stove in the corner. He poured three mugs full and distributed them before pulling up a chair and sitting down in front of the desk beside Bois Sec. The old man sipped while quietly eyeing first one and then the other. Bois Sec sipped and almost gagged. He had never tasted a more hideous mixture. It smelled like coffee, but the mixture of tastes was impossible to separate. Old Amos saw his surprise and explained.

114

"It's coffee, right enough. A Frenchman got to have his coffee. But I'm a *remède* man too. I has to take the right herbs to stay young and healthy. I make a herb tea and flavors it up so it tastes good. The coffee taste is most important so I make it twice as strong as ordinary to kill the herb taste. I like things spicy so I put in a garlic pod and a couple of pepper pods, then I put in my own special recipe of herbs to ward off the *jermiads*. I ain't telling what herbs I use. That's a *remède* man's secret. I pour oil over the top to keep it from boiling over. Everybody knows if coffee boils it gets bitter."

Among the other tastes was a definite bitter taste that lingered even after the heat of the pepper subsided. Bois Sec only pretended to sip from his cup after the first taste. The small amount he took was enough to give him a more than fair idea of what the foul concoction tasted like. BoBo continued to sip slowly while Amos drank his portion down and indicated that he wanted a refill. BoBo accommodated him and then changed the subject to the purpose of his long trip.

"I come to see you on special business and you're the onliest man in the world can help me."

Amos seemed bored and preoccupied as BoBo continued.

"I got me a map that shows a place I need to get to. It's a place called Pont Diable. I don't know what it's called now."

Amos jerked straight up at the name of Pont Diable.

"Ain't nobody needs to get to that place. I know it right enough. Nobody goes there. You're right, nobody but me knows where it is so it ain't got no name at all as far as anybody's concerned. I knew a few went, or tried to go, a good many years ago, but no good ever come of it."

As BoBo had begun to suspect, Amos' behavior at the door had been deliberate and calculated to discourage the intruders. It was not the result of a disordered mind. Bois Sec wondered if the herb tea had suddenly cleared the old man's mind.

"It's no need my asking you what you want to go out there for. They's just one thing makes a man take leave of his senses after he hears what you must have heard about that place and still leaves him thinking he's got to go on anyway. I know from the old stories that nobody's around to remember it but me. I thought about going out and digging myself before I got so old, but without a map a body could spend the rest of his life poking around and not come up with anything — and that's not the kind of place a man wants to spend the rest of his life in. Even if you know exactly where you want to go and you goes in and gets the job done and gets right out, you've been in there too long. They's strange, purely unnatural things goes on in there — things even a *remède* man such as myself don't want to face. I don't know why I should go out of my way to help you go out and do yourselves in."

BoBo looked straight at the old man and interrupted. "Listen here, Amos, you know as well as anything that after coming this far there ain't no turning back till I've got what I'm after or till I'm satisfied it can't be had. You can make it easy or hard. If you want to make it easy I can lay a little something on you to make it worth your while. If you don't help there ain't much we can do except go on and try to find it on our own."

"I was just talking to the wind. I know there ain't no human way to talk you out of a digging. I hope you got a good map." The old man shook his head almost sadly.

BoBo produced the ancient parchment from the folds of his shirt and drew forth the gold piece from his pocket. He pushed them across the desk to Amos. No explanation was necessary. Amos hitched his oversized spectacles higher on his nose and held the coin, almost touching the lens for a close inspection.

"Uh-huh, *ahn*. Oh, it's been a long time since I seen one of these, a long, long time — way before the big blow in '56. Two men come in just like you. That's been thirty-seven years ago. I guess they got caught in the hurricane on the swamp. Never seen or heard from them since, but that wasn't too unusual at the time. A lot of people weren't seen or heard from again after the wind. Yeah, they had a piece just like this. I ain't likely to forget. I seen a few before. Somebody would find one washed up on the beach or somewhere. It's the real thing, all right. I don't guess you'd be telling me how you come on this? It might help if I knowed."

BoBo told him as briefly as possible about their encounter with the old woman of the swamp. Amos listened intently to the story. Every so often he would nod his head and smile. The smile could be detected by the movement of his cheeks. His mouth was invisible under the mustache.

"*Ahn,* so you've met Marie? Mad Marie, I come

117

to call her. Mad about one thing . . . getting to that treasure. I figured she'd be dead by now. She must figure she's hexed or something or she'd be in there herself. Why she ain't got herself killed I'll never know. I've heerd tell that the spirits go easy with people that's a little tetched in the head. Leastways it must be so in her case.

"Most people don't come back after one trip to the Pont. I know at least twice she's went and I don't know if she's sent somebody else in. I don't think she'd know what to do with the loot after she got it now. When she's a few years younger she had big ideas what she'd do if she got rich — but that was then. Now she's too old and set in her swamp ways for it to do her any good. She's just set on gettin' it for the sake of gettin' it now. I reckon she thinks she can beat the devil and his spirits if she can somehow get that treasure away from him. It's a personal thing, her against whatever it is out there keeps people from coming back."

He shook his head and contemplated before continuing. "I couldn't tell a body for sure just what it is guarding the place. I just know the stories I've heard about that place in particular and swamp spirits in general. I could make spells against what is, but I don't know if what I could do would help against what it is out there guarding that spot. They must be a powerful zombie around there with pretty strong medicine. A spirit is likely to start wandering anywheres a person is put away with a proper funeral. And when that person is a evil person to begin with, that spirit is bound to be evil. They weren't anybody as evil as some of them who sailed with Jean Laffite,

118

so it just stands to reason that he's a bad zombie even as zombies go. From what I gather, he's pretty bad about turning people into *loups garous*. Sometimes the peoples come back, sometimes they don't. When they do, they don't remember anything about what happened.

"They's a old woman on over to Galliano knows what I mean. Her old man walked off into the swamp one day and didn't come back. Next day a peculiar red fox shows up and just sits there looking at her from out by the chicken house. She wasn't one to be skittish of wild critters, but she said something about that particular fox spooked her. Mebe it was his hair. It was the same peculiar shade of red as her husband's. Anyway, next day she goes out and there he is again, big as life sitting there like he knowed her. This went on for three or four days till it got so she got the jitters ever time she went out there to gather in the eggs. He didn't bother the chickens or suck the eggs or nothing else bad you'd normal expect a fox to do. He just showed up and stared at the old lady.

"Finally, she got so she couldn't took it no more, so she takes a butcher knife and goes out when she knows he'll be there. She goes up closer than she'd been to him before and still the fox didn't move. He just kept on a staring. She said his eyes looked almost human, but she was bound and determined to get shut of him so she got as close as she dared and throwed that butcher knife as hard and as fast as she could. He looked surprised and hurt when he jumped out of the way — almost, that is. The knife nicked his back leg pretty bad before he excaped.

119

"The ol' fox didn't make it back the next day, but along towards sundown who should come limping in from the swamp but her old man. Said he'd hurt his leg when the ax slipped while he was chopping wood, but she noticed he didn't have the ax with him. When she tried to get him to tell all about it he just looked confused like he couldn't remember what had took place. She knowed in her mind, though, what happened. She'd swear up and down that he'd come back as a *loups garous* in the form of a fox."

Before BoBo and Bois Sec could let that story sink in, another started. "That ain't the only such story," Amos began.

"A few years back it wasn't unusual for trappers and hunters to catch something that would have a peculiar expression or look out of the eye or way of doing that was like some friend or cousin that had gone missing not too long before. People won't hardly hunt anywhere's near there anymore. And after somebody goes missing, which happens every year or so, people gets awful careful about how they hunt. If it was just a regular ol' zombie, I think I could unhex him. But I don't know about what it is up there. I would try, of course, but I can't give no guarantees. About the only way I never heard of a *loups garous* getting unhexed is when he goes back to where he was before he was hexed and coming in contact with somebody there who's got the gift. That old woman in Galliano must have had some of the gift and just didn't realize it.

"Most critters don't have the reasoning of a fox to get back to the right place. Most of them just keeps on wandering. I imagine most of them gets their reasoning back for a little while from time to time, which must be pretty awful. Or mebe they keeps some of their reasoning and knows that if they go back they's just likely to be hunted down."

BoBo wondered what had given the old man such remarkable insight to the thinking of a *loups garous*. Did he really have a gift that would give him such knowledge, or was he speaking from experience? He did not press the point.

The old man continued. "What I'd like to do is talk you out of the whole treasure hunt."

He stopped and peered over his glasses at BoBo. BoBo did not answer. He just looked straight back at the old man and shook his head.

Chapter 13

The Map

Amos carefully unfolded the map and bent so low his nose was only inches from its surface. He moved the lamp closer and peered in silence through the thick lens for what seemed to Bois Sec an impossibly long time. Every so often he paused and nodded or shook his head, as though he were involved in a deep problem whose solution at times seemed within his grasp and then it would slip away.

Bois Sec let his attention wander over the room while Amos continued to pore over the map. One entire wall was shelved from floor to ceiling. The shelves contained an odd assortment of bottles, boxes, bags and cans. Each was labeled with strange picture writing that could have been deciphered only by the old man. A dozen or so dusty, ancient books, notebooks, and loose yellowing papers lay flat on one of the lower shelves.

The wall directly behind the desk was almost

covered with everything imaginable that could be pinned on a flat surface — yellow, crumbling pieces of paper, faded photographs, bits of string, hair, feathers, tufts of fur, and other unidentifiable objects. In places the wall contained several thicknesses of pinned scraps. A large, peculiar looking stuffed bird with molting gray feathers sat on a peg projecting from the center of the wall. The desk top was like a combination of the shelves and the wall.

The outside wall was heavily draped except for a small opening, the same one they had seen showing light from the ground below.

Bois Sec was becoming more and more restless as the minutes stretched into an hour or more. He glanced back at the stuffed bird. It appeared to have changed position slightly. He stared at the stuffed creature and it appeared to stare back with fierce beady black eyes. It appeared to move again, and he realized that the unsteady flame from the lamp was creating the illusion by casting long, moving shadows.

At last Amos nodded his head more vigorously than before and looked up with emphasis. He motioned BoBo over and they both bent over the map. The old man spoke in a hoarse whisper as he pointed with a thin white finger to various features on the map. BoBo would question Amos in the same tone of voice.

At first Bois Sec tried to catch a few words they were saying, but he couldn't understand enough to make sense. He tuned them out and returned his attention to the molting gray bird. He tried to conduct a staring contest, but the bird won. He tried to imag-

125

ine the bird moving, and it seemed to work as the light played with the form and shadows. He tried by sheer force of will to make the bird jump from its perch to the center of the desk to break up the long meeting. However, the bird sat stolidly on, staring with his unflinching solemn gaze into Bois Sec's eyes until the boy's glance shifted.

Bois Sec was almost to the point of getting up and disturbing the two, which would have been unforgivable, when BoBo and Amos rose as if on a signal. The old man was still talking and gesturing as he took something from his desk drawer and something else from the shelf and put both into a small cloth bag, which he gave to BoBo. BoBo reached over and folded the map and put it in his pocket with the *gri gri* bag. He picked up the gold coin still lying on the desk, but in response to a gesture from the old man he put it back down. Amos took it and slid it into a desk drawer in an instant.

Amos smiled with his eyes and became more cordial than he had since the two had arrived. He hastened around the desk, shook hands with both of them, and said, "Good luck to both of you. Now, you mind what I said. If you do exactly like I say you might just make it. Whatever you do, don't get caught out there after dark. Get started early in the morning and you should get out in time. Get out early enough even if you have to leave some behind. I think it's a good idea to forget the whole thing and go home because I ain't giving any guarantees you're gonna make it even with the *gri gri* I give you."

He picked up the lamp and led the way toward the front door. It seemed to take less time to leave than it had to enter. Amos held the lamp at the door while BoBo lit the lantern. Without another word he stepped back inside and slammed the door.

The night sounds of the swamp took over as they made their way back toward the boat. Bois Sec looked back just before they entered the heavy brush. The dim light was flickering again from the corner window. An ever-so-slight chill shook his body. He turned to follow BoBo.

Chapter 14

Through the
Haunted Swamp

Neither slept very well that night. The entire venture had seemed vague and unreal until after the meeting with Amos Boudreaux. His presence as much as his words had made them more aware of the unknown forces active on Pont Diable.

Bois Sec dreamed the old woman of the swamp was hovering over him. Once Minette appeared to look down at him mired on his back in a thick, gummy substance. She started to reach down then recoiled in horror and ran away screaming into the distance. The echoes of her screams jerked him to wakefulness, then dissolved into the eerie sound of a screech owl somewhere in the swamp.

BoBo thought he might be foolish to challenge forces so beyond him — all to satisfy his pride. He had gotten along well enough for all those years by taking certain precautions to avoid conflict with

those beings out there beyond the real world. He remembered all the frightening ghost stories he'd
heard from childhood. They now achieved a terrify-
ing new dimension. He knew, though, that if he gave
in to his fears they would run his life in the future. If
he were alone, the decision to abandon his venture
would be easier. Bois Sec, he thought, could never
look up to a man who ran from his fears.

The world looked better when the sun came up.
After a hearty breakfast rounded off with coffee,
BoBo was almost jolly. But a certain underlying ten-
sion seemed to hang in the air. Bois Sec noticed that
the swamp sounds didn't lessen as much as usual
with the rising sun. The birds were more active, and
he saw more seagulls than was usual for this far inland. The creatures of the swamp appeared nervous
and restless. He dismissed it as imagination. The
sky was cloudless and not a trace of breeze stirred
the leaves as they started on their way. His preoccu-
pation with the surrounding swamp soon disappeared as he had to devote his full attention to keeping the boat in the channel.

The little boat wound through a hopeless maze of
narrow, overgrown waterways to emerge into open
marshland. Barataria Bay could be seen near the horizon, but BoBo turned long before they reached open
water. For some hours they wandered, edging ever
closer back toward the heavier inland growth.

BoBo kept his attention on the wall of green until he spotted a landmark apparent only to him. Bois
Sec saw nothing to distinguish one point from any
other when BoBo directed the boat toward a spot
that looked like solid growth. Amos had instructed

him well. They seemed to be heading for a hopeless tangle when a channel appeared through the thick foliage. In reality a thin veil covered the opening.

They moved into a tunnel of perpetual gloom. Long, twisted branches reached out from the tangle of trees as if grasping for the boat and its passengers. The tree trunks appeared to have struggled forth into an agonized, tortured existence. Heavy, drooping masses of gray green Spanish moss hung ghost-like from above. The atmosphere was hot, humid, and deathly still, but Bois Sec found it hard to suppress a shiver. He had never seen the swamp so oppressive. It had always seemed friendly before. Now it seemed like a living aggressive being, grasping with gray tentacles for a victim.

In the hazy distance he saw a small flickering light dancing through the greenery. It lasted a few moments then disappeared as quickly as it came. BoBo had seen it too. He paled and became very serious.

"Old Amos told me about that. Might not be nothing, might be a *feu follet*. In any case it's a bad first sign. A *feu follet* is just about the most unpredictable spirit they is. They's so fast you never know where they'll show up next."

He dug in his pocket and brought out the cloth bag given him by Amos. He attached a bag of powdered substance, a small polished metal disk and a carved wooden emblem to a leather thong and handed it to Bois Sec, then fixed another one for himself.

"Tie that *gri gri* bag around your neck. Be sure the disk is out where it can catch the light. That's the only thing I know that can scare off a *feu follet*. He sees his own light reflected and thinks it's another one like himself. They don't like one another's company, so he real quick moves on somewhere else. I wish the other spirits were that easy to distract."

He was annoyed at himself for giving in again to the old superstitions, but he wanted to take no chances until they faced whatever awaited them on the Pont. If he could meet the challenge there, he could throw away all his *gri gri* forever.

They had both heard that the strange dancing lights in the deep swamp were merely glowing phosphorescent swamp gases. But they had heard many more stories connecting the lights to the spirit world. This was not the time to take chances.

The banks, which at most had been low, fell away gradually and then disappeared entirely. As far ahead as they could see there was no ground — only water with a thick growth of cypress and vines. The vegetation was almost as dense and oppressive as before, but occasional patches of sky could be seen.

It was more difficult to stay within a channel with no banks to guide them. After brushing a mud bank just beneath the surface, Bois Sec went forward with a weighted line to take soundings of the bottom so they wouldn't go aground. With the boat barely moving through thick water, the air seemed charged with an electric energy. Swamp creatures appeared restless and distracted. A squirrel darted one way and the other on a branch overhead. He paused briefly to look at the boat then continued his pointless movement. He made no attempt, as squirrels usually do, to stay on the side of the tree oppo-

131

site an intruder. It was as though he were frightened of something much greater than man.

BoBo was getting restless at the slowdown. It seemed forever to Bois Sec before spots of muddy ground could be seen rising above the water. The areas of land showed more and more until they were once again traveling between solid banks.

BoBo increased the speed to a little more than dead slow. "We lost too much time in the cypress swamp, but if we'd got ourselves lost or stranded on a mud bank we might of been this time tomorrow getting out. This is one place I don't want to stay any longer than we have to. Something about this place gives me the shakes. I ain't never been in the swamp that made me feel like this. I sure would like to get out before night, but I don't know how we'll make it after losing all that time. There ain't no way we could make it back across that cypress swamp with no banks to guide us in the dark."

Bois Sec was glad to hear the voice of his uncle. It seemed to add a touch of security. He answered, "I noticed that myself. We can't see the sky enough to tell whether clouds are building up or not, but I figure our problem is more with what's on the ground than what's in the sky."

The foliage pressed in so close from both sides and above that there was scarcely space for the boat to squeeze through. The sky was completely obscured. They were moving through a twilight tunnel of gloomy green filtered light. Strange animal sounds could be heard from the depths beyond the green walls on either side. A rustling, shuffling noise became apparent on both banks very near the boat.

133

The noise grew closer and more intense and was accompanied by the sound of faint clickings, as though the swamp itself had come alive and was preparing to engulf the little craft.

Bois Sec was becoming inwardly terrified when BoBo unexpectedly broke into laughter and explained, "There's a lot of sounds out there I don't know what is, but that sound I've heard before. They's land crabs. I don't know what they're doing so restless this time of day and this far from the beach, but look close and you'll see."

Sure enough, when Bois Sec peered deep into the brush on the bank he could see the movements of hundreds of large, yellow crabs shuffling along, bumping and clicking on the ground under the plant life. He was relieved when they passed through the large colony a few minutes later.

BoBo continued, "I can see why people down on Gran Isle calls them ghost crabs. I know the first time I heard them it was early morning before daybreak and they woke me up from camping out on the beach. Gave me a pretty good scare till I saw what it was. A lot of people down there eat them. Don't seem worth the trouble to me. They're not nearly as tasty as water crabs — there ain't as much meat, and you have to work harder to get it."

"I don't think I'd care to try 'em myself," said Bois Sec. They looked anything but appetizing to him.

The light was getting dimmer but it was not the kind of darkness that comes at the end of day. The foliage stood out in sharp detail in a strange half-light. The tops of the trees moved ever so slightly, as though beckoning to some force that could not be seen from ground level. In the distance was a low muffled rumble that could have been thunder. Bois Sec's imagination told him it was something else.

BoBo looked worried but no less determined to continue.

Through the tangle ahead a towering black shadow began to take shape. As they moved closer, the trunk and gnarled branches of a giant cypress tree materialized from the shadow. The drooping Spanish moss suspended from the branches looked like the tattered remnants of rotting clothes hanging from long, grasping arms. Bois Sec looked deep into the gray film. He thought for a moment he had seen the face of the old woman peering from its depths, but it was only a knotty formation on the trunk of the tree where two branches came together.

"We're just about there!" shouted BoBo. "That's the first landmark ol' Amos mentioned. We're gonna have to step lively now. Throw a line up there and I'll catch this stump back here. We'll have to beat our way on foot from here on. There should be a rise just beyond the cypress with more solid ground. Step fast in that direction or you'll bog down."

He handed Bois Sec a heavy burlap bag and a machete, picked up a shovel and pick for himself, and took a long step to the bank. Bois Sec didn't step quite far enough. He felt himself sinking in a bog that seemed to have no bottom. He was waist deep in the mire before BoBo's strong hands caught his shoulders. BoBo's boots were breaking through the thin crust of earth over the mud before Bois Sec was out. They both had to move fast to firmer ground.

136

The undergrowth made every step an obstacle course. They took turns hacking brush with the machete. The distant rumblings were coming closer and sounding more definite. The upper branches of trees were swaying in a wind that filtered down to a breeze where the two hacked their way toward the cypress landmark. The higher ground near the large tree didn't have as much growth, so the pair could move more rapidly. However, on reaching it, BoBo found the greenery still too thick to allow him to spot the second cypress and the oak tree that was supposed to be nearby.

"I'm afraid you're gonna have to climb up and have a closer look," he told Bois Sec. "We could tramp around and find it, but we don't need to waste no more time than we have to. Here, let me give you a boost."

Bois Sec had already started trying to shimmy up the trunk, but it was too large and the first branch too high to allow him success. With an assist he made the first limb and in a matter of moments he was high in the branches. Bayou boys learn early about such things as tree climbing. Bois Sec had the added push of fear and desire to be through with the whole treasure hunt.

He strained to see through the rapidly darkening swamp then climbed still higher to get a clearer view. As he climbed above lower surrounding treetops, he felt a strong breeze. A gust almost loosened his hold.

"I think I see it!" he shouted down. "It's over yonder way," he pointed. "It's all dead and just about stripped down to the trunk, but it must be what we're looking for because it's the tallest cypress around and they's a big oak tree just to the right of it." He looked upward and said, "I can see what's making it get dark. There's one hell of a storm rolling in from the Gulf. Solid black all acrost the sky."

"It's probably just a thunderstorm. Hurry on down and let's take care of our business and get out of here." BoBo lied as much to himself as to Bois Sec. It wasn't likely that a mere thunderstorm was coming from the Gulf this time of year, particularly after all the signs he had been seeing all day: the behavior of the swamp animals, the electric atmosphere, the strange light. He was so intent on completing their mission that he refused to see the obvious. Besides, he knew that there was really no place to run that would be much safer than their present location. He experienced a tightening around his middle, a feeling of being at the mercy of overwhelming unmerciful powers.

He still had mixed beliefs about most of the stories of spirits loose in the swamps. He wanted to reject them, but it was hard to dismiss something that had been part of him since childhood. Those superstitions had been part of the swamps for years before he was born. If he survived the next few hours, he knew he would be free as he had never been before.

A tropical hurricane was not a tale or superstition. It was a fact. Was it possible that the spirits in this particular swamp were so powerful that they could bring down the wrath of the skies?

Chapter 15

Digging for Treasure

BoBo was having second thoughts but nothing would stop him now.

Bois Sec didn't sense any indecision on the part of his *nonc*. His only doubts were of himself and his ability to keep up with BoBo when the real trial came. He sensed that there was something bigger than a summer storm facing them.

They hurried on in the direction Bois Sec had indicated from the tree. Although the underbrush was thinner, it seemed to reach out at every opportunity to snag clothing, catch a boot, or push against the body to hold them back. Heavy clouds were beginning to darken the sky overhead, and the sharp crack of thunder following flashes of lightning seemed very close. Large, scattered drops of rain fell.

The second cypress trunk extended upward like a gigantic bone. The weathered gray white was broken into jagged points against the sky. The lower

part spread into bony roots grasping long, twisted fingers into the earth. The longest root finger pointed toward a spreading oak tree nearby. It seemed to be struggling to emerge from under a shroud of gray moss that weighted its branches to the ground. The rising wind gave movement to the moss to create the illusion of a large creature under the gray shroud, writhing and struggling to free himself. The illusion was heightened by the tortured moan of the wind blowing through the hollow trunk of the nearby cypress. The effect was so real and the timing so exact that both explorers doubted there was any illusion involved. Bois Sec was convinced that supernatural forces were involved. He had lost all enthusiasm for treasure hunting.

BoBo was wavering inside, but his outward actions showed no loss of resolve. He knew that if they gave up now he would be bothered the rest of his life or until he returned.

He cleared a rough path as quickly as possible between the two trees and paced the distance twice. The second time he marked a point halfway between the two. The steadily developing downpour turned into sheets of wind-driven rain. The darkening sky was brightened by almost continuous flashes of lightning, dancing from one horizon to the other.

BoBo had to shout to make himself heard. "I'll take the shovel and you take the pick. We gotta probe all around my stake till we find the marker. It's a big flat rock that should be lying right on top of whatever's buried. Hit it straight down pretty deep. The ground's pretty firm up here, but chances are it's sunk some in a hundred years."

They probed in a widening circle around BoBo's stake. The ground was becoming muddier by the minute. They slipped and slid in the muck while fumbling with tools that didn't seem up to the task. After they had widened the circle to a radius longer than the combined length of their bodies, BoBo paused. "If the map is right it's got to be somewhere in this circle. Let's start back and probe a little deeper this time."

Bois Sec's shouted reply was almost lost in the rumble of thunder and the sound of wind. "Why don't we make it back to the boat or crawl under that big old oak tree till the storm blows over? You got the spot marked and we can come back later. It should let up in a few minutes."

BoBo knew the storm would not lessen in a few minutes. "No, let's stay with it a little while longer. Start pokin'."

They attacked the muddy circle with more determination, driving the slime-coated tools as deep as human power would permit with each stroke.

"Hey, I think I got something!" Bois Sec shouted. BoBo rushed over to uncover the find. A few shovelfuls revealed the rounded top of a root. After BoBo uncovered two more roots, Bois Sec's pick rasped against something solid. This time BoBo's shovel uncovered something flat and hard. The mud and water made it difficult to wrestle the flat slab of a stone out of the hole. They both ached from the exertion and finally laid the stone on the ground beside the hole.

The sun had retreated to a safe haven behind a cloak of black clouds to wait out the storm. The only light came from the storm itself as its electric bolts flashed across the sky.

BoBo splashed water from the hole onto the stone and wiped with grimy hands to find out if they had the right stone. A flash of lightning revealed what his hand had already discovered — a small Roman cross carved on top. He forgot his exhaustion when he picked up the shovel to renew his attack on the hole. For every two shovelfuls he displaced, one would slide back in from the crumbling sides. Rain washing into the hole dissolved the mud at the bottom. They found it necessary to take turns shoveling mud and bailing slush. Progress was slow.

The wind increased in gusts. Each gust subsided after a few seconds, but the main continuing force of the wind was always greater after a gust than before.

Less than knee deep, the shovel scraped against a small but lengthy solid object.

"I hit a stick or something here . . ." BoBo shouted. "Hold it, there's another one . . . and a ball-shaped thing here. Let's get our hands muddy and see what we got so far."

They lowered themselves to hands and knees in the slippery mud to clean the hole out. A few flashes of light revealed what they had uncovered.

Bois Sec was frozen stiff at the sight of a skull grinning grotesquely from its final resting place. A bony arm held a twisted hand in front of exposed ribs as though trying to ward off a blow. Lodged between two ribs and extending upward between fleshless fingers, the remains of a broken blade caught a reflected gleam of light.

144

The scene was lit for only a second — but the afterimage lingered on. Bois Sec could still see the ghostly scene in the blackness. Even closing his eyes would not erase the sight of the terrible grinning apparition.

BoBo shook him by the shoulders. When he spoke there was urgency in his voice. "Come on and get your wits back. It ain't nothing but some old bones. They can't hurt you."

There was no getting through to the boy. He continued to sit unmoving in the mud beside the hole. BoBo gave up and started removing the bones himself. He quickly and carefully stacked them on the side opposite Bois Sec, then resumed digging and bailing. Exhaustion and determination overcame his fear. The closeness of the goal waiting just beyond his fingertips gave him strength to continue past his normal limits.

The area was almost constantly lit by the lightning. At times it seemed to fill the entire sky. The noise of the storm would have made conversation impossible, even if BoBo had had the strength to shout and if Bois Sec had been in a frame of mind to understand. They made a strange picture: BoBo struggling against the resisting but gradually deepening hole, and his unmoving audience — the skeleton on one side and a terrified Bois Sec on the other.

The sound of metal scraping against metal cut through the turmoil of surrounding sounds and BoBo charged the hole with renewed fury. His efforts soon revealed the top of what appeared to be a large sea chest.

He scraped furiously around the edge of the

shape to uncover the latch. An oversized rusty lock proved unyielding against repeated pounding with the shovel. He tossed the shovel aside and grasped the pick. It was impossible to get enough leverage to force the lock. In angry desperation he pounded the top of the container. To his surprise, the rusty metal gave in to the force of the pick. A few more ripping blows revealed the contents.

The raging storm was forgotten for a moment. Even Bois Sec revived at the sight in the flickering light. Neither could resist the impulse to thrust his hands into the glittering heap. Gold has a feel unlike any other metal, with substantial heaviness to suggest its value. They were awed by the presence of so much of the substance that had been an irresistible magnet to man since the first golden flecks were discovered thousands of years before.

BoBo grabbed the burlap bag from Bois Sec's belt and started putting great handfuls of coins through the opening as fast as his hands could move. They would have to make several trips to transport all the treasure to the boat.

His work was interrupted by a blinding flash followed almost immediately by an ear-bursting report.

It was some moments before BoBo recovered from the shock of the lightning bolt. The smell of burning sulphur still filled his nostrils when he looked over for Bois Sec.

He was gone.

Chapter 16

Flight through the Hurricane

Where Bois Sec had sat there was now a large bullfrog squatting and staring impassively ahead. It was difficult to be sure in the uncertain light, particularly after having his vision affected by the lightning strike, but there seemed to be something familiar about the frog's expression. When he realized what the frog reminded him of, a different kind of fear — a sick fear — seized him.

He forgot for a moment all his dreams of becoming a rich man. His concern for his younger partner overcame all other considerations. He did not know for sure how to cancel a spell once it had been cast, but one thing he could be certain of — the sooner he took himself and this thing Bois Sec had become out of here, the better his chances would be of seeing the situation return to normal.

He grabbed the frog before the pitiful creature

could realize what was happening and tossed it inside the bag with the gold.

As soon as BoBo jumped from the partial protection of the hole, the full force of the wind hit him. He made no attempt to recover the tools. He made three running steps down the slope with the wind to his back when a gust hit him square in the rear at the moment both his feet were off the ground. It tumbled him end over end and slammed him rolling and sliding back to earth. He lost his breath and some skin, but he kept a tight hold on the mouth of the bag.

He lay on the ground for a few moments, catching his breath, while the gust subsided. He kept holding the bag opening with one hand and checked the welfare of the frog with the other by feeling from outside the bag. The frog was still kicking and the gold was still clanking, so he pushed himself to his feet. He proceeded quickly but with more caution.

Back at the excavation site, while BoBo was making his flight, the skeleton had begun to move. It rolled and slid slowly toward its final resting place in the hole on top of the gold. It was as if it had completed its task of guarding the gold and was now returning to its post as sentinel over the precious metal. The freshly dug earth continued to wash away from under the skeleton, allowing it to slide back to its former position in the hole. It settled in almost the same position as it had been found earlier by the two treasure hunters. The mud continued to slide back over the treasure and its grotesque guardian until there was only a slight depression to show where the digging had taken place.

Meanwhile, BoBo continued to fight his way toward the boat. Long years of experience in the swamp had given him a cat-like sense of direction. After he had once traveled over a particular piece of ground he could almost retrace the route blindfolded. The talent served him well because most of the landmarks that had guided him to the treasure had been changed in the wind, rain, and darkness.

The water level was rising rapidly below the ridge. From ankle deep it very quickly became knee deep as he pushed toward the lower ground near the bayou. Deeper water and thicker underbrush made movement more difficult with every step. Branches seemed to deliberately reach out to bar his way or snag his clothing or grab arms and legs. The greenery seemed more aggressive now than it had earlier because of darkness and his haste to beat the rising water. Several times the bag was snagged. Once he had to use both hands and the weight of his body to pull loose the valuable package.

Heavy burlap is remarkably durable, but the weight of more than fifty pounds of gold coins pushing against the weakened fibers began to have its effect. As a few strands of the coarsely woven material parted, more strain was placed on the remaining fibers. First one ravel then two and more developed. Still the sturdy bag retained its treasure.

When a hooked barb on a swinging branch caught the seam of the bag, BoBo hardly noticed the slight tug. The seam weakened and pulled apart slowly, more with each jogging, sloshing step of a man pushed past the point of fatigue, a man fighting

for survival. In his physical and mental state BoBo did not notice as the precious coins gradually slipped through the widening opening in the side of the bag to be gulped into thick, rising swamp mud.

He would run, trip, struggle to his feet, run some more, then trip again in his frantic effort to get out of the swamp. Through all his struggles he maintained a vise-like hold on the bag. The water was waist deep and rising when a flash of lightning showed the familiar shape of the boat through the foliage just ahead.

BoBo knew that what remained of the bank near the boat would be soft and crumbling, so he cautiously worked his way near the boat by holding tight to branches with each advancing step. He waited momentarily for another bright flash and saw what he was looking for to help him aboard. One branch forking out over the boat appeared to have the thickness to support his weight.

He clawed his way through the underbrush to the base of the tree from which the branch grew. The water was chest deep as he pulled himself into the tree, still holding on to his precious bag. Twice the wind almost forced him back into the swamp, but he continued dragging himself onward until he was safely over the deck and dropped from the branch. The distance to the deck was not far when he turned loose. His weight had pulled the limb down until its leaves were brushing the railing. He lay where he fell, still holding the bag tightly.

The strength returned quickly to his rawhide-tough body. When he tried to stand, the wind pounded him against the bulkhead. He lost his footing and had to make his way on hands and knees to the door of the cabin. It was only after he was inside and the door was latched that he released his hold on the burlap bag. He still did not realize that it was empty. The sturdy little boat creaked and groaned against the force of the deafening wind outside, but it held together.

He slid to the floor beside the fallen bag and reached over to examine its contents.

He couldn't believe what his hands told him. He felt every inch of the bag's interior and found only two coins tangled in the raveled thread at the bottom. Again and again he felt inside the bag as though expecting the treasure and the frog to reappear by magic as he supposed its contents had disappeared. When his hand slipped through the large open seam, he realized that magic may not have been involved. He leaned back against the wall, clutching the two remaining coins in his hand. He pounded his clenched fist against the deck in helpless frustration.

The loss of the gold he could endure. Good fortune came and went — boys didn't.

Why had he involved Bois Sec in anything so uncertain? He could easily have left him with *Maman* Guidry. She had as much as asked him to stay. Sure he would have protested, but he would have gotten over it. BoBo had grown more attached than he realized to his little companion. He felt drained and empty inside. He would have cried, but he was so exhausted that tears would not come. He sat silent

154

and numb. He did not move as the storm continued its raging fury outside.

Time passed. Minutes turned to hours, and still he sat unmoving, oblivious to the surrounding turmoil.

A new gust of wind rocked the boat then started to subside. In a matter of minutes, the storm had quieted to a stillness that hung over the interior of the cabin like a heavy woolen blanket.

Chapter 17

The Reunion

"I thought that storm would never stop!" The familiar voice came from somewhere near the far corner of the cabin. It continued, "It seemed for sure the whole boat was coming apart a board at a time."

"Hey, lil buddy, where you at?" BoBo shouted.

He leaped to his feet and fumbled with the matches, trying to light the lantern. He had to confirm with his eyes what his ears told him. Sure enough, there in the corner, unwinding himself from a tarpaulin covering, was the missing Bois Sec.

The boy had never seen his uncle so emotional. He was laughing and crying at the same time when he wrapped his arms around Bois Sec and swung him around several times before releasing him.

"Watch it, you're breaking my ribs. You're some kind of sorry looking mess anyway." They stood apart and laughed at the sight they presented. Both were caked with mud, scratched, and their clothes were hanging in shreds.

"I'm sure glad that storm's over. I ain't ever seen one that bad," Bois Sec said.

"I've got news for you, partner," BoBo replied. "We've just been through half a storm. We're in the eye of a hurricane and it won't last too much longer. We'd better check the deck quick while it's quiet. It won't be so bad this time, not having to be out in it. Chances are, if this old boat stood up to it once it can do it again."

They hastened outside to check the moorings. The lines were all secure, but BoBo reinforced them with new rope from the cabin. The barrels had all broken loose and the deck was littered with an assortment of debris from the swamp. Other than that, the craft was in good shape.

"Everything's okay out here. Let's go back inside and get cleaned up and put some coffee on," BoBo said. A stiff breeze was rocking the boat from the opposite direction before they settled down with steaming hot coffee cups. They felt better in fresh clothes and with warm stomachs. They could even laugh about the experience as the wind quickly picked up in intensity.

"What happened to you out there? One minute you was there and the next time I looked up you were nowhere in sight." BoBo didn't mention the frog.

"I'll have to say I was pretty scared when them bones showed up. I kept looking and I swear it looked like they was moving theirselves even after you threwed them out of the hole and up on the

157

bank. Then you opened up the box and it kinda brought me back to my senses seeing all that gold. I hadn't no more than got a good handful in my pocket when it seemed like the whole world blew up. From where I sat it looked like the lightning hit you direct. I was blinded, I guess, and without really thinking about what I was doing I jumped up and found myself running.

"I don't know how I ever found my way back or got on the boat when I did. It was like a dream when things go on happening in spite of everything you do to change them. I found the boat and I jumped out and caught a mooring line and I was pulling myself hand over hand up the line onto the boat. I don't remember nothin' else till I find myself all rolled up under the tarp listening to the storm." He stopped for a moment, then added, "It sure looks like I ran out when the going got tough."

BoBo replied, "You ain't got nothin' to be ashamed of, boy — or should I start calling you man? I wasn't thinking a bit clearer. Sometimes when your body realizes that you're going to die if you don't do something fast it takes over from your reasoning. That's called an instinct for survival. Only the mother instinct is as strong. If we'd messed around and fumbled through trying to help each other, we would both probably be dead back in the swamp. That same instinct told each of us that the other was able to take care of hisself, so each of us did what he had to do to survive." He reasoned that it was best not to confuse the issue by mentioning the ridiculous episode with the frog. He changed the subject.

"You say you got a handful of gold? Did you get back to the boat with it?"

"Yeah, it was still in my pocket when I changed clothes. Here, I'll show you." He picked up the muddy trousers and removed eight glittering coins from the pocket.

"With the two I got we're gonna do a little better than come out even. That's not bad for a few days' work," BoBo laughed, then added, "Here, hold my coffee cup. There's something I got to do before the storm starts building up too much."

He left the cabin and went to the rocking deck. He grasped the *gri gri* bag containing the magic charms old Amos had carefully formulated to ward off evil spirits, and removed it from the string around his neck. Then he threw the bag with its "magic" contents as far as he could in the direction of the treasure cache.

He felt a new sense of freedom when he returned to the cabin.

The roar of the rebuilding storm soon made normal conversation impossible. They had another cup of coffee before BoBo extinguished the fire. BoBo turned down the wick on the lantern and they wrapped up secure in their blankets while the storm continued.

Long before the storm had blown itself out hours later, they both slept.

A Message from the Deep Swamp

Sacre! Did you think that was the end,
bon ami? Well, there is more —
but only for those who are brave
enough to go on.
If you don't feel that brave,
put the book down and go fishing.
If you want to continue, read on.
But BEWARE!
The feu follets may
be up to their tricks again . . .

When BoBo and Bois Sec awoke
after a long rest, the houseboat was
moving. It was not the gentle movement of a moored vessel, but a fast
movement on open water. They rushed
outside to discover that the lines securing
the houseboat to the bank had been cut.

They were adrift near a large body of water which
BoBo deduced must be Barataria Bay.

That canceled their plans to go back for the rest
of the treasure. They were several hours and countless channels away from the treasure site. BoBo
would have to use the treasure map to retrace the
route with its many twists and turns. During the lull
in the storm, they had placed the ten gold pieces in
two equal stacks on top of the map on the table.

When BoBo reached for the map where he had
left it, it was gone. Also missing was one of the
stacks of gold. Maman Guidry's note and the directions to old Amos' house were still on the table.

"BoBo, that ol' swamp woman said she was
gonna come back and collect her half of the gold. Do
you just reckon . . ." Bois Sec's voice trailed off.

Strange things happen in the deep swamp, but
what the boy suggested was impossible. When BoBo
spoke it wasn't to answer Bois Sec's question. "I
don't guess I could ever find my way back to the treasure without that map. The onlyest thing I can figure is we go back to ol' Amos Boudreaux and see can
he redraw the map."

They found ol' Amos' house the same as before.
BoBo banged the big iron knocker. The sound echoed

162

deep within the chambers, but no one answered.

Again and again he knocked, but all was silent.

He pushed gently on the door and it swung open. The air was damp and musty. Everything was covered with cobwebs and dust.

They entered the room where ol' Amos had pored over the map before. It looked the same — material tacked to the walls, shelves filled with dusty bottles and *gri gri* objects, the stuffed bird still on his perch above the tall chair.

The next sight was absolutely unbelievable.

There was Amos Boudreaux. Or what had once been Amos Boudreaux.

The yellowing skeleton could have been in the ancient high-backed chair for years. It still wore the thick, square spectacles. The old nightgown hung in tattered, ragged fragments from the bony frame. A bony finger pointed toward the front of the desk.

BoBo and Bois Sec didn't tarry to look for an explanation. In less time than it takes to tell about it, they were outside. Only a few moments later, they were rowing toward the houseboat.

Neither spoke. Sometimes there are no words or explanations that fit.

Strange things happen in the deep swamp. Strange things indeed.

Words to Know

apparition: a ghostly figure; a strange appearance
appease: to satisfy; to give what is demanded
au lait: with milk
barter: to trade goods instead of using money
bebes: (Cajun) babies
bon ami: (Cajun) good friend
booty: goods or valuable items that have been taken or
   seized
brawny: strong and muscular
Bronze John: yellow fever
bulkhead: an upright partition that divides a ship into
   compartments
burré: (Cajun) a card game
cache: a place for hiding goods or valuables
Cajun: a native of Louisiana believed to be descended
   from the French Acadians; their language and
   customs have, over the years, been spiced with
   English, Spanish, Indian and other influences, to
   make it a distinctly unique culture.
cher: (Cajun) a term of endearment; dear
connoisseur: a person who is very well informed about
   a particular matter of taste
expedition: a journey undertaken with a specific
   objective in mind
fais-do-do: (Cajun) a Cajun dance/party
feu follets: (Cajun) playful swamp spirits

165

foliage: cluster of plants, branches, etc.

futility: uselessness

grandmere: (Cajun) grandmother

grandpere: (Cajun) grandfather

grenier: (Cajun) a small upstairs room for the young single man

gri gri: (Cajun) a bag of magic potions to appease spirits

isolation: being separate from others, totally alone

jermiads: (Cajun) mild sickness; stomachache

joie de vivre: joy of living

jumping the broom: (Cajun) a temporary wedding ceremony that will suffice until the priest comes to town

lagniappe: a small gift given by a store owner in appreciation for a purchase

le jeune file: (Cajun) young, pretty girl

loups garous: (Cajun) an evil swamp spirit that takes the form of an animal

maman: (Cajun) mother or matron

nankeen: (Cajun) kerchief

nonc: (Cajun) uncle

oblivious: completely unaware

oppressive: difficult to bear; harsh

patina: a sheen, usually bronze-like, produced by age

pirogue: canoe made from a hollowed tree trunk

produce: collective farm products

remède **man:** (Cajun) medicine man who has powers to cure

Sacre!: an exclamation, similar to Gosh! or Wow!

skeptical: doubting or questioning

skiff: a flat-bottomed, open boat

snipe: an imaginary bird/animal

soundings: measured depths of water

supernatural: pertaining to powers outside the natural world

tante: (Cajun) aunt

tepid: lukewarm or weak, without body or flavor

ti: (Cajun) term of endearment (from pe<u>ti</u>te)

tingaling: (Cajun) musical triangle struck with a
metal rod to give a "tingaling" sound

trey: a three on a card, die, or domino

unique: one of a kind; unlike any other

vegetation: plants covering an area

voison: (Cajun) neighbor

zombie: a corpse revived by voodoo

About the Author

JAMES RICE has illustrated dozens of popular children's books, most of which he also wrote. The native Texan, born in Coleman County, Texas, holds a B.F.A. degree from the University of Texas, a master's in education from Howard Payne College, and an M.F.A. from Stephen F. Austin University. He has taught both art and music at the high school and college levels, and has commanded quite a following with his illustrations and books. Rice and his wife, who live in Hico, Texas, have five children and seven grandchildren.